THE KING'S TREASURE

by
Mark Ramsay

A SIGNET BOOK
NEW AMERICAN LIBRARY
TIMES MIRROR

*For Sonya Beth,
her brother Richard,
and their parents, with love*

NAL BOOKS ARE AVAILABLE AT QUANTITY DISCOUNTS
WHEN USED TO PROMOTE PRODUCTS OR SERVICES. FOR
INFORMATION PLEASE WRITE TO PREMIUM MARKETING DIVISION,
THE NEW AMERICAN LIBRARY, INC., 1633 BROADWAY,
NEW YORK, NEW YORK 10019.

The first chapter of this book appeared in *The Bloody Cross*,
the third volume of this series.

SIGNET TRADEMARK REG. U.S. PAT. OFF. AND FOREIGN COUNTRIES
REGISTERED TRADEMARK—MARCA REGISTRADA
HECHO EN CHICAGO, U.S.A.

SIGNET, SIGNET CLASSICS, MENTOR, PLUME, MERIDIAN and NAL
BOOKS are published by The New American Library, Inc.,
1633 Broadway, New York, New York 10019

First Printing, March, 1983

1 2 3 4 5 6 7 8 9

PRINTED IN THE UNITED STATES OF AMERICA

ONE

The long column of mounted men snaked its way down the side of the ravine and into the mist. The ravine was a singularly evil-looking place. Dark, tangled foliage overhung the bank, and matted bracken grew down the sides. The bottom of the ravine was obscured in fog. The path was so narrow that the horses had to place each hoof directly before the other, and the wagons were in imminent danger of tumbling into the gorge. A potbellied, one-eyed old man walked ahead of the wagons and directed their drivers as they inched their way down the path. Most of the old man's words were some kind of blasphemy or obscenity.

A few hundred paces down, the path widened and two men rode side by side. One was hideously ugly, with a face so scarred by sword cuts that it seemed to be made up of the ill-matched parts of several faces. One of his ears was missing. The other man was younger and sandy-haired, and at his saddle he carried a morningstar: a spiked ball attached to a wooden handle by two feet of chain.

"Where are Draco and Wulf?" asked the ugly one. His name was Donal MacFergus, and he had an ax ready at his own saddle. Both men wore shirts of mail and helmets.

"They must be ahead of us, farther down," said the other. He was called Simon the Monk, because he had spent several years in a monastery before becoming a soldier. "They started down ahead of us, and there's no way we could have passed them on that path."

"I don't know," said Donal uneasily, as he looked about him. The fog was now too dense to penetrate more than a few feet. "Strange things happen in fog. Spirits move about in fog that fear the daylight. They can trick you."

"Oh, cease your prattle of spirits," said the other uncomfortably. "This isn't Ireland, you know." All the same, Simon's eyes were a little wider as he scanned the fog.

Down in the densest and darkest of the mist, two more riders led the procession. They inched along, their mounts feeling a slow way down toward the sound of running water. Thick ropes and skeins of fog twisted and swirled around them like a basket of writhing serpents.

"Have you ever seen such stuff?" asked the one with yellow hair spilling out from under his helmet. "By Jesus, if the devil were a spider, this would be his cobweb!"

The other said nothing, but he kept turning his head from side to side. From his conical helmet a steel nasal slanted down to protect his nose, and from either side of the nasal his flint-gray eyes stared fixedly. The eyes were all that was visible of his face, for the rest was hidden beneath a veil of iron mesh. The veil continued downward to join a long coat of mail that dropped below the rider's knees. It had long, tightly fitted sleeves to the wrists, and his hands were covered with thick black

2

leather gloves which were studded on their backs with short iron spikes.

His name was Draco Falcon. He was owner, captain, and lord of this little army of some two hundred men, which he now feared to be hopelessly lost. While one hand held his rein, the other rested on the hilt of a long, curved sword which hung at his belt. He thought he saw a shadow flit in the mist below.

"What was that?" said the yellow-haired man.

"I don't know," Falcon said, "but I saw it, too."

The younger man loosened the short sword at his waist. His name was Wulf, short for Aethelwulf Ecgbehrtsson. His sword was short, broad, and curved, and a small shield was hung from its scabbard. He wore a short sleeveless vest of mail in addition to his steel cap. He hated fog as much as anyone.

"Grendel used to walk in the fog," Wulf said. "He'd sneak up to the hall at Heorot and break in the doors and snatch up the sleeping thegns. He'd bite their heads off and hold their carcasses over his head like wineskins while he drank their blood."

"I'm more worried about men than about monsters," Falcon said. "I've been a soldier long enough to know a fine ambush site when I see one." His voice was slightly muffled by the cloth-lined veil of mail over his mouth.

There were more of the flitting shadows. Were they men? What else would they be? He had traveled more than most men, and had always been assured, wherever he went, that nearby there were giants, fabulous beasts, werewolves, vampires, or the like. Nevertheless, in spite of all these assurances, he had never encountered a single example of the supernatural.

"If they're men," Wulf said, "they'll know better than to attack a force the size of ours."

"How are they to know how many of us there are?"

3

Falcon asked. "If they see only two men, they'll probably attack." Neither assumed that the men might be friendly. Nobody lurked in fog with good intentions. In any case, strangers were always assumed to be hostile until proved otherwise.

There were noises now that did not seem to be caused by the river that flowed sluggishly at the bottom of the ravine. There was a clatter of rocks and an unmistakable clink of metal. "Get ready," Falcon muttered. He reached down and freed his long, kite-shaped shield from its place at his saddle. His left forearm went through its straps, and he tightened them until he was satisfied with the shield's fit.

"Keep your back toward the bank," Falcon advised. It would help keep most of the enemy in front, if it came to a fight. The path had now debouched onto a narrow bench of land between the river and the slope of the ravine. The water shone black as old blood. The growth along its bank was thick but sickly-looking, and no trace of froth marked its surface.

"This looks like a dragon's lair," Wulf said, "a haunt for orcs and nixies and nicors."

"Keep your mind on more dangerous things," Falcon said. "I've not encountered a dragon yet, but men are another matter. We'll wait here until the rest of the men—" The first rock clanged from his helmet. Falcon jerked his shield up to protect his face. The mail would keep him from being cut, but a rock could still smash bones through the flexible armor.

Wulf cursed as a stone struck his thigh. He jumped from his horse and darted into the fog. The horse stayed where it was, afraid to move in the obscuring mist. A rock struck Falcon's horse on the neck, and it reared. As soon as he had the beast under control, Falcon dismounted. Trying to fight mounted was futile under such cir-

4

cumstances. Shield held high, Falcon stood with his back to the bank, awaiting his enemies. He did not have long to wait.

A few more stones rattled off his shield, then the hidden men attacked. He had an impression of long, unkempt hair, swirling beards, snarling teeth, and ragged clothes. One swung at him with a heavy wooden club, but Falcon took him out of action with a short cut to the wrist. The man howled and dropped his club. Falcon's long, curved sword was meant to be used with both hands, but it was possible to utilize it one-handed as long as really powerful blows were not necessary. Another man charged with a stone tied to a stick. Falcon cut the man's thigh, and he beat a limping retreat. As long as the attackers were as poorly armed and unarmored as this, he should have no difficulty in holding out until his men arrived.

Then the others confronted him. They were big men in full mail, and there were at least six of them. They loomed in the fog like giants. Falcon released the handhold of his shield and slipped his forearm from the forearm strap, letting the shield dangle from his shoulder by the guige strap. This way, it afforded his left side some protection while he used the sword with both hands.

The first to the attack wore a long hauberk of mail and a flat-topped helmet with a nasal. His shield was small and oval and it bore no device. This man was a good deal more of an opponent than the first ones. He bore a sword, long and straight. The blade was notched, but Falcon knew that it could cut grievously nonetheless. The wielder essayed an overhand cut at the helm to draw the shield upward, but Falcon did not respond. In the midst of the stroke, the mailed man cut low, to sever the knee tendon. Falcon merely dipped his shoulder, and the long point of the shield intercepted the blade.

The frustrated warrior tried a high cut at the neck, but by that time Falcon had picked his point of aim and brought the broad, curved blade up and into the armpit of his enemy's hauberk, where the intricate tailoring of the mail links made a weak spot. The unusual blade split the opposing rings and cut into the muscles and nerves of his enemy. The sword dropped, the man screamed, and Falcon wheeled to face the rest of his opponents.

There were too many of them. Some wore the long mail hauberks of knights: knee-length, with sleeves to the wrist or elbow. They had mail covering their heads and helmets with nasal bars. None wore the face-covering helms that were now popular but restricted hearing and sight.

A man roared and charged. He held his shield high, and Falcon dropped and slashed low, carving a leg from under the man. There was a bitten-off grunt as the man fell. Then another warrior was there, his spear held at a menacing angle. Falcon backed toward the cliff. He knew from long, hard experience that a man with a spear could be far more dangerous than any swordsman. The man feinted high, and Falcon flexed his shoulder to take the point. The spearman raised his point and went in over the shield at the neck.

Falcon dropped to the ground. This man was deadly. His opponent stabbed at him repeatedly, but Falcon drew as much of himself as he could beneath his shield. He made a small cut to the ankle. His opponent skipped back at the last possible instant. Another came in swinging with a mace. Falcon brought the curved sword across horizontally at waist level. It did not split the man's mail, but the blow was powerful enough to drop

6

him, retching. The spearman took advantage of the distraction to try another attack.

Falcon struck the spearpoint upward with the crescent hilt of his sword, then brought the blade across and down in an oblique cut that split the spearman from shoulder to waist.

Wulf was still stumbling about in the fog. His small shield was insufficient to protect him from the flying rocks, so he sought to close with his enemies and deal with them using his falchion. The short, curved blade was ideal for this sort of close-quarter fighting, but the damned fog was so confusing that he was unsure in which direction to charge. Two ragged attackers appeared, and he ducked beneath their crude weapons and gutted both of them with a single horizontal stroke. Then there was a man in armor who wore a face-covering helm and carried an ax. Wulf dove for the ground. He heard the ax whistle over his head, then he got his feet beneath him and sprang to his full height, bringing the blade up between the other man's legs and splitting him to the navel.

Another rock bounced off his steel cap. Wulf was ready to howl with frustration. Where were the rest of the men? Another enemy appeared before him. This one wore a long hauberk and mail hose and a face-covering helm. He gripped a long sword in both hands. This could be tricky. A man so completely armored had few weak spots. Wulf got his back as close as possible to the steep bank so that he could devote his full attention to dealing with the knight.

The armored man came in swinging, and at that moment Wulf knew that this was no knight. The man was obviously unused to the weight of his armor, and he did not allow for the sag and sway of the iron fabric, which shifted the wearer's center of balance. The man tried a blow which should have taken Wulf's head off, but he missed by several inches.

Wulf timed his move carefully and ducked beneath the next blow, coming up behind his enemy and swinging his blade. There was no sense in dulling his edge against the heavy mail, so he cracked the man across the shoulders with the flat. The mailed bandit whirled clumsily, and Wulf danced back. The armored man burst into an oxlike charge, sword held high for a stroke calculated to split Wulf from crown to crotch. At the last possible instant, Wulf danced nimbly aside and let the man lumber past, giving him a boot in his mailed backside for further impetus. The man took several lurching steps and saw that he was headed straight for the riverbank. He tried to halt himself, but he had built up too much momentum in his heavy mail. He tottered for a horror-stricken moment, then fell into the water with a tremendous splash. He sank in his iron like a kettle full of bricks.

Wulf ran for the bank, and three more of the ragged men tried to block him. He cursed and turned, running back along the level ground to where he could hear the sounds of Falcon dealing with his attackers.

Donal and Simon heard the sounds of battle long before they could do anything about it. They cursed the treacherous path that restrained them to a slow walk. It was clear from the sounds that their companions were battling outrageously superior numbers. They knew that they faced the disgrace of feudal soldiers who allowed their masters to be killed without aiding them. Simon called back up the line of men that there was fighting ahead, and he could hear the clatter of weapons being readied.

At last, they found themselves at the bottom of the path. "Where are you, my lord?" Donal called through trumpeted hands. Then he saw the familiar shaggy form of Wulf darting from one wall of fog to another. "This way," he cried, and the rest of the men followed him into the obscurity. Donal had his ax in his hand, its wrist thong securing it. Behind him, he heard the rhythmic clicking of Simon's morningstar as the ex-monk whirled the spiked ball in circles around the haft. This kept the swing of the ball under his control. It also confused the enemy as to where the attack would come from.

They burst upon the scene of the action just as some twenty bandits were closing in upon the two beleaguered men, who now stood back-to-back, menacing the encircling bandits with their stained weapons. The two horsemen split, Donal to the left and Simon to the right, plying their weapons to both sides, lopping limbs and scattering brains with each stroke. The bandits milled about uncertainly. Then a group of horsemen and footmen arrived, howling and striking, and the bandits broke and fled.

Falcon and Wulf stood breathing heavily while the men mopped up. "Watch yourselves!" Falcon shouted. "They'll hide in this damned fog and try to pick you off!"

The men stayed together in small bands as they scoured the riverbank in both directions. They dragged the bodies back to where Falcon stood for systematic looting. No man tried to take anything for himself, for Falcon's discipline was strict and expulsion from the band was the punishment for withholding loot.

The gloom of the gorge began to lighten as the late-morning sun burned away the fog. In the light, the fearsome attackers presented a less intimidating appearance. Most were filthy men in rags, no more than serfs who had armed themselves with any makeshift weapon they could. The armored men were either degraded knights or peasants who had stolen their gear from ambushed warriors. The mail was rusty, the helms dented and in poor repair, even the swords were rusted and stained, any gold or jewels once inlaid on their hilts long since gouged out.

Nevertheless, iron was valuable and always in short supply. The mail could be cleaned and refurbished by tumbling in a barrel with gravel, sand, and vinegar. Even the broken weapons and split helms could be sold to smiths as scrap. Wulf led a party to where the heavily armored man had fallen into the water, and they prodded the river with spear shafts until they located him, then dragged the corpse ashore.

Falcon's men were experienced and efficient, and when they were finished only the most verminous rags and hides were left with the bodies. As a final touch, Donal went among the corpses methodically hacking the heads off with his ax and piling them in a neat pyramid. He had long since explained to Falcon that this was an ancient Irish custom and was supposed to placate spirits or ancestors or some such. In any case, it would serve as a salutary warning to the next band of outlaws to use this as an ambush spot.

When all the loot was packed away and the weapons safely down from the gorge path, Falcon ordered the men to remount. Unlike most armies of the time, Falcon's was entirely mounted. Even the men who fought on foot rode into action. Falcon believed in mobility. For the same reason, he did not tolerate the usual train of camp followers that slowed most armies to a crawl.

They rode downstream for most of the day. Gradually, the river valley widened until they were riding in a broad, pleasant river bottom with grassy meadows, which were probably fine pasture in the spring but were now deserted with the onset of winter. The grass was close-cropped from last summer's pasturage, and brown from the advancing year.

Falcon looked up at the sky. It was darkening again, this time with high, fluff-bottomed clouds that portended snow.

"How long till the Feast of Nativity?" Falcon asked Simon, who rode beside him. The ex-monk counted laboriously on his fingers.

"Four weeks and odd days," Simon said.

"Then we're in for an early snow," Falcon said, gazing upward. Just their luck to be caught in a heavy snow in the mountain valleys. It was more than an inconvenience. It could be deadly.

Once again, Falcon questioned his wisdom in accepting this commission. He was to escort a treasure from Limoges to Cahors, across the Auvergne Mountains, in winter. King Richard of England had died trying to wrest the treasure from the Viscount of Limoges. The mission was to be kept a strict secret, of course, but Falcon knew how difficult it was to keep secrets where treasure was concerned.

The viscount was a suspicious man. He had agreed to the contract Falcon proposed, but he was not keeping the treasure in Limoges. Instead, it was in a small castle here in Limousin. The castle was on land that the viscount claimed, but the land was now technically English territory. Since the new King John of England was a monarch of little account, this borderland belonged to any who could hold it. Under heavy secrecy, the viscount had sent the treasure to the castle, which had been built by an ancestor and had been deserted for a generation or more. Falcon had been directed to take this unlikely route to the castle, once more for reasons of secrecy.

By the end of the day, they had the castle in sight.

One look told Falcon why it had been abandoned for so long. It was of a very antiquated design: a single stone-and-timber tower surrounded by a circular earthenwork rampart. The rampart had once been topped by a timber palisade, but the logs had long since been scavenged. A man standing atop the tower blew a trumpet, and several men issued from the interior. They mounted and rode out to meet the newcomers.

Falcon signaled for his standard-bearer to unfurl the banner. The big Spanish knight who had that duty complied, and the Falcon banner flapped in the chill wind. Against a background stitched with silver thread, it depicted a black falcon with wings spread. In its talons, the falcon gripped blue lightning bolts.

Ahead of the other horsemen from the castle rode a tall, bearded man in mail of good quality. His coif was down and he wore no helm, but it hung ready at his saddle. In disputed territory, a man was best advised to be cautious. He halted a few paces from Falcon.

"You would be Sir Draco Falcon, I take it?" the man said.

"I'm Falcon."

"Good. We've been expecting you the last few days. I'm Sir Rauf de Chaluz. Come with me to the castle. We've gotten some sheep and pigs and a few fowl from the local peasants. At least we can offer you a decent meal before you set out in the morning."

"Excellent," Falcon said. "We've been living on cheese and hard bread and salted fish for days." The prospect of real food was cheering.

They rode through the gateless gap in the rampart and into the bailey, the open field between the rampart and the tower. In the bailey, servants were bustling, slaughtering the livestock for dinner. Falcon directed his men to pitch their tents, for the tower was far too small to hold them all. The standard-bearer, Ruy Ortiz, began posting sentries on the rampart.

"The land's in dispute, but we're not at war," Sir Rauf said. "I keep a man on watch up in the towers. Sentries aren't necessary."

"My men are always under wartime discipline," Falcon answered. "We post sentries, and the men stay under arms."

Wulf came to take Falcon's horse, and Sir Rauf led him up the man-made mound atop which the castle stood. A short flight of steps led up the wall to a landing on the second story. The castle had no openings at ground level. A wooden bridge crossed from the landing to another ten feet away. From the second landing, a low door allowed entrance to the tower. Under attack, the bridge could be drawn up, leaving no access to the tower. The bridge smelled of fresh-cut wood. Rauf's men must have replaced it when they arrived.

The inside of the tower was pitch-black. At Rauf's call, a man appeared on a flight of steps with a torch, and by its smoky light Rauf led Falcon up and into a large room which had once been the castle's great hall. In a castle, the walls got thinner as one went higher, so the largest rooms were always on the upper floors.

In the room, Falcon could see several strong chests, all locked and the keyholes covered with lead. The lead was impressed with the viscount's seal. "Any idea what's in the chests?" Falcon asked.

Sir Rauf shook his head. "None. Only the viscount and his most trusted henchmen know. Rumors are rife, though."

"They always are," Falcon observed. "What do these rumors say?"

"Some hold that it's an old Viking hoard. Others say it's a pagan idol of solid gold. You know how men talk.

13

Whatever it is, I'll be damned glad to get it off my hands."

"I can't blame you," Falcon said. "Has absolute secrecy been maintained?"

"As far as I know. The men I've brought here know, of course, but they're completely trustworthy. Even so, I'm to keep them here for a week after you've left."

Falcon grunted. He'd lost count of the "absolutely trustworthy" men he'd known who had turned traitor.

"Come upstairs for some wine," Sir Rauf invited. Falcon followed the knight up the stairs and into another room. This one was well lighted, because it had originally had a wooden roof which was now gone. About half of the roof had been replaced, and a section of the roofed-over area was screened off with tenting. Several men were gathered around an improvised hearth, where a fire burned and wine was being heated. One of the men poured a cup of the mulled wine and handed it to Falcon. The man wore a priest's plain cassock. He was big and he walked heavily, although he did not seem fat. He made a slight clicking noise as he walked, and Falcon glanced down to see mail-clad feet strapped with spurs of plain steel.

"This is Bishop LaCru. He will be accompanying you to oversee the papal tithe."

"Nobody said anything about a churchman being along," Falcon protested.

"Nevertheless, he must go," Rauf said.

"I assure you, Sir Draco," LaCru said, "I shall not be a burden or a hindrance." Falcon shrugged. At least the man looked as if he could take care of himself.

At that moment, there was a stirring from the curtained-off section, and a hand parted the cloth to reveal a richly clad figure in the opening. It was a woman. Her face, framed by coif and wimple, was beautiful, with

14

straight, classically modeled features and black, level brows. Small and slender, she carried herself regally, her manner haughty, but the tight fit of her gown revealed a full figure. She gazed at Falcon now with large brown eyes, returning his own stare.

"This is Lady Constance," Sir Rauf announced. "She is the viscount's niece. She will also be going along with you."

TWO

"This is unacceptable!" Falcon barked. "The bishop I will tolerate. He has the look of a soldier and I needn't spare any attention from my duties for his welfare. This lady, though, will take special handling. I'll have to detail men to protect her should bandits attack. She'll have a train of servants, I take it?"

"I am quite capable of speaking for myself, sir knight," Lady Constance said. Her voice was as arrogant as her looks. "I have my maid, Suzanne, and my groom and two other servants. Not a princely establishment, you will agree."

"Five more mouths to feed, lady," Falcon said. "Five more noncombatants to slow our progress without adding to the strength of the band."

"Slow you down, will we?" Lady Constance said scornfully. "Carrying this great heap of metal in wagons, did you expect to fly?"

Falcon stared wryly into his wine. The woman had a sharp tongue. Worse, she was right. The best they could hope to manage was a slow walk.

"I concede your point, lady, but my contract said nothing about escorting a woman along with the treasure."

"Just what does your contract say?" Lady Constance asked.

Falcon reached into the pouch that hung at his belt and drew forth a small scroll from which dangled two wax seals on ribbons. He unrolled it and began to read. He was very proud of this contract. Traditionally, feudal obligation was recognized by the swearing of cumbersome oaths. Falcon had come up with the idea of sidestepping this tedious procedure by putting the terms of service in writing and having both parties affix their seals to it. As far as he knew, this had never been done before.

He reached the salient passage: "He whose seal is affixed below, Sir Draco Falcon, agrees to undertake at the pleasure of the Viscount of Limoges the escort and conveyance of such goods as the aforesaid viscount shall deem proper and deliver it safe, with seals unbroken, to the castle of the aforesaid viscount's cousin, Maurice de Burgh, at Cahors." Falcon rolled up the contract and put it back in his pouch. "Nothing about any lady," he said.

"Nothing about any treasure, either," Lady Constance pointed out. "Only 'goods' were mentioned. I am obviously part of the goods."

"Lady," Falcon said, fuming. "I feel that my goodwill is being taken advantage of."

"Nothing has been taken advantage of, Sir Draco, unless it be your inability to understand just what you've agreed to."

"Sir!" said Bishop LaCru. "Madame!" He looked at both of them sternly. "I pray you cease this unseemly bickering. We are about to undertake a long journey through much danger in a most unpleasant season. It would be best if we could at least start out friends." He turned to Falcon. "Sir Draco, you are a knight and therefore pledged to protect ladies of high birth under the laws of chivalry."

Falcon glared at him. Unlike most knights, he held the cult of chivalry in low esteem.

"My lady," LaCru said, "I think Sir Draco is justified in feeling some dismay that his duties will include some which he had not anticipated."

Falcon decided to put the best face on an inescapable situation, and said with as much grace as he could muster: "Lady, I crave your pardon for my hasty words. We've had a long journey and we had a sharp fight with some outlaws this morning. It may be that my tongue has run somewhat ahead of my better nature."

Apparently mollified, Lady Constance said: "And I crave yours, Sir Draco. My confessor has often chided me for my swift temper and warned me to curb my speech."

Bishop LaCru smiled, and the air of tension left the room. Falcon raised his cup and drank, looking at Lady Constance. Overbearing bitch, he thought. He could swear he read similarly hostile sentiments in her eyes.

Falcon had left his helmet thonged to his saddle, but his coif was still up. He had lowered the iron veil, the aventail, to drink, and now he pushed the coif back so that it dangled between his shoulders. The others studied him intently. Draco Falcon was a striking man.

It was not so much his handsome, hawklike features that commanded attention, but his singular, almost bizarre coloration. His face was burned dark brown from his years in Palestine, and his abundant straight hair was raven-wing black. From his brow to his nape, a broad streak of white ran through his hair. From his hairline at the base of the streak, a thin white line ran down his forehead and crossed his left eyebrow, whitening the eyebrow where it crossed. The line continued down the eyelids to the cheek, thence down to the jawline and neck, to disappear beneath the mail hauberk. Several men in the room turned away to cross themselves and mutter spells against the evil eye, for they knew that no natural agency could mark a man thus.

Falcon was a big, rangy man of about thirty-two. His shoulders were wide, but even within the bulk of his uncommonly fine hauberk, the tight-drawn sword belt defined a narrow waist and lean hips. His hands were big and scarred and plated with callus. His flint-pale eyes and white teeth were startling in so dark a face. The fact that he had all his teeth was a matter of some wonder. Unlike peasants, the young noblemen of Europe were raised on meat and milk and cheese, all conducive to good teeth, but hard training with weapons usually cost them a good many by the time they were dubbed knight, and warfare generally accounted for more. A full set of teeth was the sign of a man who knew how to use his shield.

Except for the eyes and his height, Constance thought, he might almost be a Saracen. Then, unwillingly, she thought, God, but he's a handsome figure of a man! Hard and arrogant of course, but then, what knight wasn't? None of these thoughts showed in the imperious expression of her face.

I pity the man who marries this one, Falcon thought. Fine face and figure, though. And she's not one of those colorless fainting ladies the poets are always singing about. I'll wager she could take charge of a castle under siege as well as bear children without fuss, and she's probably tireless in bed. He looked at her over the rim of his cup as if it were the edge of a shield.

Wulf came into the room carrying a bag of oiled leather and helped Falcon peel out of his mail. The other knights in the room came over to admire the fine armor.

19

The hauberk was rather old-fashioned, coming down to below the knees and with sleeves to the wrist, but the links were far smaller than those to be found on European mail. Moreover, the thickness of the rings was evenly tapered so that the chest, shoulders, and belly received the greatest protection. The rings over the back and arms, and the skirts, were made of thinner wire, for a great saving in weight. The hauberk weighed about a third what a European one, made of hammered iron wire of the same thickness throughout, would have.

"Saracen mail," Sir Rauf commented. "Finest I've seen."

"You were a Crusader, Sir Draco?" asked LaCru.

"Once," Falcon said.

"Your sword is Saracen, too, is it not?" LaCru went on. "I've never seen its like. May I have a closer look?"

Falcon drew the great blade from its sheath. The blade was uncommonly long, a bit more than three feet, slightly curved and somewhat broader near the tip than at the hilt. The guard was a great bronze crescent, and the pommel was a smaller crescent of the same metal. The sharkskin-covered grip was long enough for a two-handed hold. It was not the design of the unusual sword that excited the admiration of the men in the room, however. It was the coloration of the blade, which was mottled and streaked like woodgrain, in a beautiful pattern of contrasting silvers and grays.

"Damascus, by St. Denis!" swore a knight.

"I've never seen a Damascus blade so large!" exclaimed LaCru. "Surely this is not the work of mortal hands."

"Has it a name?" asked Sir Rauf.

"In the East she's called Three Moons," Falcon answered. "I renamed her Nemesis."

"Nemesis," fused LaCru. "Was that not the name the heathen Greeks gave to their goddess of vengeance?"

"It was," Falcon said.

"I've always heard that the true Damascus is sharp beyond the common run of blades," Sir Rauf said. "Is your Nemesis keen?"

"Wulf," Falcon said. The Saxon bent and picked up a straw from the floor and held it up. The blade flashed across and down almost lazily, with no real force. The straw parted. Falcon sheathed the blade in a single motion, without looking down at the scabbard.

Bishop LaCru took the straw from Wulf and examined it closely. It was cut on a bias, as neat as the point of a quill pen. "I couldn't have done that with a razor," he remarked.

Constance simmered slowly, ignored. Men were always making such a fuss over their swords and horses and armor. They acted as if there were nothing of importance in the world except hunting and fighting. Once in a while they'd compose a love poem, but that was only to be fashionable. Even in their poems, they usually contrived to display their love by fighting. In any case, the object of their devotion was always some unattainable lady to be worshiped like the Blessed Virgin, never desired as something as prosaic as a wife.

As the sky darkened, the servants brought up joints of roasted meat and steaming loaves. The men all sat on the floor and ate voraciously. Lady Constance and her maid retired to the screened-off section to eat, making for a more comfortable atmosphere. When a lady was present there were always silly formalities to observe, and soldiers on service had little patience with such things.

"Where is this Lady Constance headed?" Falcon asked Sir Rauf.

"She's being sent to meet her husband in Italy," Rauf said.

"So the viscount stretches his investment in my services by having me provide an escort for his niece." Falcon could see that he would have to be more careful about the wording of these contracts in the future.

As soon as the eastern sky began to lighten, Falcon saw to the marching order of his little army. In the center were three wagons loaded with the treasure, whatever it might be. Other wagons contained tents, provisions for the men, their personal possessions, and the all-important fodder for the horses. One wagon was set up as mobile quarters for Lady Constance and her maid.

Falcon gathered his officers for their day's assignments as the men stood by their mounts, waiting for the order to move out. "Ruy," he said to the big Spanish knight, "take the banner and your squadron to the front as advance guard. Rudolph," he went on, turning toward an Austrian knight, "you and your men have the rear guard today. Donal," he said to the Irishman, "take all the footmen and keep them near the wagons. Guido," he continued, and a small Italian in leather jerkin and steel cap stood up from where he had been squatting, "I want you and your crossbowmen and the two Welsh archers riding on the wagons. Leave your horses with the remounts. I want you personally to ride on Lady Constance's wagon. If any of the men offers to molest her, kill him."

"Yes, my lord," Guido said.

"Where shall I ride, Sir Draco?" asked Bishop LaCru.

"Where you will. I presume your commission is to keep an eye on the chests, so I suggest you stay near them. If there's to be any fighting, that's where it will happen, in any case."

Falcon turned to the old one-eyed master engineer, Rupert Foul-Mouth. "Are the chests stowed and secured properly?" he demanded.

"Tight as the devil's prong up a priest's backside," Rupert said. LaCru's face began to turn red.

"Get used to it, my lord bishop," Falcon said. "Rupert has a way with words." He waved to Wulf, and the Saxon blew a long blast on his hunting horn. Falcon's officers strode off, barking orders at the men under their command. Within minutes, the men were mounted, arranged in their assigned marching order, and ready to move out.

Falcon mounted his own destrier and surveyed the men. Satisfied that all was in order, he waved to Ruy Ortiz, and the Spaniard rode out of the bailey with the falcon banner held high. At proper intervals, the rest of the train moved out. LaCru rode up beside Falcon. The bishop was now helmeted, and his shield hung from his saddle.

"Your men are well disciplined, Sir Draco," said the prelate. "I was with Richard Plantagenet's army in Palestine for a while. Richard was a great soldier, but even his men didn't move like this. You must drill them like the Greek emperor's soldiers."

"I do," Falcon said. "I wanted an army of soldiers, not warriors, and that's what I've created. Even my knights know how to obey orders."

LaCru shook his head with wonder at the idea of disciplined knights. The advance guard was now out of the enclosure. With a popping of whips, the heavy-laden wagons lurched into motion. They creaked and groaned in protest. The wagons were small, each drawn by a brace of oxen. Rupert had insisted that nothing larger would be able to negotiate the mountain trails they must follow. Rupert also insisted that they were sturdy enough to bear the weight and make the journey. Falcon had never known Rupert to be wrong about equipment he had built himself, so Falcon was satisfied with the assessment.

Falcon and Wulf followed the wagons, leaving Rudolph and the rear guard to leave the bailey last. They turned to return the waves of Sir Rauf and his men.

"Think they'll hold their tongues?" Falcon said.

"I fully expect them to," LaCru said. "The Viscount of Limoges is not tolerant of lapses in his subordinates."

"What do you know of the land we must cross?" Falcon asked the bishop.

"Most of it's in dispute," the prelate answered. "That means it's alive with runaway serfs and deserters from everybody's armies. A number of knights have seized castles and set themselves up as robber-landlords. There are some monasteries, but I could not tell you whether the monks have stayed or fled."

"Splendid prospect," Falcon said. They rode until midday, when Falcon called a halt for rest and a cold meal. By sections, the men filed past a provision wagon, where they were given bread and cheese. This was another of Falcon's confusion-preventing innovations.

Falcon had Wulf summon the two Welsh brothers to where he was sitting on the ground with his back against a tree, eating his frugal lunch. The two men, Gower and Rhys ap Gwynneth, unlike the rest of Falcon's men, wore no armor or helm, nor did they carry sword, ax, or spear. Instead, each carried a huge bow as tall as himself. Their only other arms were long knives at their belts.

"Gower, Rhys," Falcon began, "you two have the sharpest eyes among us. I want you to ride out to our flanks where the ground permits, and to our rear, and find high ground where you can watch for anyone dogging us. Most especially watch the rear. You can ride in and change horses as often as necessary." The men nodded and strode off to find their mounts. Falcon pondered whether there were other precautions he should take.

Lady Constance walked toward him. She was accompanied by her maid, Suzanne, a pretty girl of about seventeen with long, thick blond braids.

"Good day, my lady," Falcon said, without bothering to rise.

"And to you, sir," she answered. "I was walking off the stiffness from that cramped wagon. I believe I shall ride my palfrey when we take the road again."

"You may if you wish, but you must stay with the wagons. We are riding through territory as dangerous as any you are likely ever to encounter, and I cannot detail men to provide a guard for you if you ride away from the train."

"I am not accustomed to being told how I may come and go," Constance said coldy.

Falcon could only stare uncomprehendingly. What kind of household had the woman been raised in? For all the songs of the troubadours, noble women were usually regarded as little more than brood mares for the purpose of producing heirs of suitable blood. Peasant women often had more freedom. "Best accustom yourself, then, lady," Falcon said. "My command is law here, and the husband you're traveling to meet will probably have similar ideas."

"No doubt," Constance spat. "He'll probably be just like you, an armored brute with his brains in his sword arm!"

"Enough!" Falcon shouted, bounding to his feet. "Get back in your wagon, or get on your horse, but cease baiting me and refrain from disturbing my men."

"And if I choose to ride as I wish?" she demanded.

"Then," Falcon said, "it shall be my very great

pleasure to order you bound and tossed into the bed of your wagon for the rest of the journey!"

Lady Constance glared about her. A number of the men were standing around, grinning. "Have these louts nothing better to do?" she demanded.

"Attend to your duties!" Falcon barked. The men straggled away, poking one another in the ribs. With a final glare, Lady Constance whirled and strode away, followed by Suzanne. Wulf passed them on his way to find Falcon, and he turned to eye Suzanne's gracefully swaying bottom as she walked by.

"Ready to ride, my lord?" Wulf asked.

"Ready," Falcon said. He saw Lady Constance mounting her palfrey. "Nothing good will come of having that woman with us," Falcon said, glowering.

"I can think of some good I could derive from it," the Saxon said, watching Suzanne climbing into the wagon.

"Don't even think of it," Falcon said. "The men are displeased as it is that I've forbidden them to bring women along as we march. If they know you're tumbling that wench while they go without, it could make for hard feelings."

"What about my own feelings?" Wulf said with a lascivious grin.

"If that's your problem," Falcon said, "you should have taken care of it back in Limoges."

"I did," Wulf protested. "But that was days ago!"

Falcon booted him in the rear. "Mount up!"

That afternoon, Falcon and Wulf rode with the advance guard. The weather was holding well, although the sky still threatened snow. Idly, Falcon drew his bow from its case behind his stirrup leather and strung it expertly. With his thumb, he tested the tension of the string. It was a fine Saracen bow, triple-curved and made of layered wood and horn and sinew. Although it was much shorter that the yew bows the two Welshmen carried, it was nearly as powerful.

"Going to do some hunting, Sir Draco?" Falcon turned and saw Lady Constance riding behind him. Beside her was Bishop LaCru. In the dead-slow pace forced by the wagons, he had not even noticed the sound of the horses nearing him.

"No, lady," he answered. "If I shot a deer with this, the arrow would be out the other side and I'd never find it again. This is a war bow."

"You, a knight, using a bow?" she said incredulously. In the West, only footmen used missile weapons.

"Sir Draco has been a Crusader, my lady," LaCru said. "In Palestine, we often used bows against the Paynim. A man could die of boredom waiting for the Saracens to come to hand strokes. They were too wily for that."

"I suppose it is proper for killing heathens," Constance said, "but surely, Sir Draco, you would not employ a bow to kill Christians, would you?" Her tone was venomously sweet.

Falcon glared around at the men of his advance guard, mentally daring them to crack a smile. All wore stony countenances more eloquent than mirth. "I always assume anyone who is trying to kill me suffers from a lack of religion, my lady." He took an arrow from his quiver and sighted along it, twirling the shaft to determine its straightness. It was perfect, and the fletching was in order. He forced himself not to look at her. "Did I not say that you were to ride with the wagons, my lady?"

"Surely I'm well protected here among the soldiers and knights of your advance guard," she said.

"For now," Falcon answered. "But if we were attacked, they must fall back on the main body. Have you ever been among knights when they are retreating, my lady?"

"I have not. What of it?"

"They have little time for the niceties. These destriers they ride would knock your little palfrey over like a lapdog standing between boarhounds and their dinner. You would be lucky if only three or four warhorses trampled you."

"I fear he's right, my lady," LaCru said. "This is no place for you."

"I am not afraid," Constance said. "I have this light of chivalry to protect me, have I not?"

"Wulf," Falcon said, "toss this woman across your saddle and throw her into her wagon. If she struggles, tie her up and sit on her."

"Keep away from me!" she warned Wulf. "Sir Draco, you wouldn't let this villein lay hands on me, would you?"

"Lady, if I thought it necessary, I'd order him to flog the hide off your back and he'd do it."

"Bishop LaCru," she protested, "you are a Christian warrior. Surely you would not stand by and see a high-born lady treated thus?"

"My lady," the bishop answered, "I took a vow of poverty, chastity, and obedience. I recall no oath of chivalry."

Falcon smiled grimly as Lady Constance pondered her choice. There was a clatter of hooves, and he looked up to see a horseman approaching at a gallop. It was Rhys ap Gwynneth, and he carried his bow strung in his hand. He drew rein beside Falcon.

"Men following, my lord."

Falcon cursed. "How many, how far back?"

"At least a hundred we could see," the Welshman reported. "All mounted, all armed."

"Now, lady," Falcon said, "perhaps you will be so good as to return to your wagon." Face pale, she nodded assent. Falcon turned to Ruy Ortiz. "Return to the main body, but slowly and in good order. A hundred men are little threat unless they get reinforcements."

"As my lord commands," said Ortiz.

"Wulf, bishop, let's go have a look at these men."

THREE

From the rise of ground where Gower ap Gwynneth sat his horse, they looked down upon the column of men who dogged their trail. The men rode at their ease, as if assured that they had plenty of time to catch up to their prey. Some were accoutered and mounted as knights. Others rode horses of varying quality. A few rode donkeys or mules. Arms and equipment varied widely, but each man had at least a spear.

"Robbers," Falcon said. "So much for the secrecy of our mission."

"Do you think they know what we carry?" LaCru asked.

"Would they be following if they did not?" Falcon said. "Nobody molests two hundred armed men unless the rewards are commensurate with the hard knocks to be had."

"Even so," LaCru pointed out, "they are too few to be any danger to us."

"Too few now," Falcon agreed. "But, as you have said, this place is alive with bandits and deserters. They'll keep picking up strength as they ride. When they have enough men, they'll attack."

"Then what shall we do?" asked LaCru.

"We'll attack first, of course," Falcon answered.

That evening, Falcon and his officers plotted strategy around the large fire in the center of their camp. Half the men remained under arms and at their sentry posts at all times. Muffled in their cloaks, the men cursed the cold, but they knew that their survival depended on alertness. Night attacks were a rarity, but desperate men might try anything.

The scouts were giving their report. Falcon had a number of foresters and poachers among his men, and they knew how to conduct a night reconnaissance.

"They're mostly gathered around five big fires," said a small English spearman. "They've got a cask of wine open, and I don't think it'll last long."

"Sentries?" Falcon asked.

"Just two men sitting a bowshot down the road in our direction. They're pulling at a wineskin, too, to keep off the cold."

"This won't be difficult," Falcon said. "There won't be one of them awake in three hours. We'll hit them at midnight."

"I advise that we wait," said Ruy Ortiz. "The ground here is treacherous and unfamiliar. We could lame some of our horses trying a night attack."

"Ruy's right, my lord," said Rudolph of Austria. "The mounts will be stepping into the coals of those fires and burning their hooves. If we attack at first light, I'll wager they'll still be sodden and the fires will be cool by that time."

Falcon agreed with the wisdom of this advice, and a dawn attack was planned. He detailed men to muffle the horses' hooves. Others were assigned the task of taking all the robbers' mounts. Last of all, he gave Donal a special mission.

"Donal, take four or five men and get me some prisoners. Not the scum, mind you, but some of those men who look like degraded knights. There must be some sort of leadership among them. I want to find out how they got word of our cargo." The Irishman nodded.

"Everyone not on duty get such rest as you can," Falcon ordered. "We'll have brisk work to do before we breakfast tomorrow."

From the treeline, Falcon surveyed the bandit camp. The light was still too dim to commence the attack, but already he could make out some details. The bandits lay sprawled wherever sleep or drunken stupor had overtaken them. The fires had ceased smoking. Most of the animals were tied to a long picket rope in a meadow nearby, but there were a dozen or so horses tethered to a small tree within the camp. A small group of men slept near the tree. These would be the ones that looked like knights.

Falcon beckoned Donal to him and pointed out the sleeping men near the horses. "I see 'em, my lord," said the Irishman. "You'll have a few of 'em to talk to anon."

The men were stripping the sacking-cloth mufflers from their horses' hooves. Bishop LaCru was near Falcon. Like most military churchmen, he carried a big wooden club, since he was forbidden to "smite with the edge of the sword," or shed blood. Properly used, the club could kill by concussion without bloodshed.

The Welshmen rejoined the band, giving Falcon the signal that they had killed the sentries with their knives. A last glance up and down the line assured Falcon that all was in readiness. The light was now strong enough for the horses to be sure of their footing, and he could see signs of stirring in the camp. He raised his arm and brought it sharply down. The blast of Wulf's horn sang out, and with a roar the line of men charged forward.

Some of the men in the camp had time to sit up and widen their eyes in horror before they were trampled. Those who managed to stand were cut down. A few escaped the first slaughter and made a dash for the horses. Those who were not run down in the attempt reached the beasts only to find Falcon's men already in charge of them. None tried to surrender. There was no such thing as mercy for a captured bandit. All tried to flee or fought to the death.

It was all over so quickly that Falcon had not even had to draw his sword. He rode once through the camp, running a few bandits down, then he was out the other side and turning. By the time he got his horse turned and back to the edge of the place where the camp had been, the mopping-up was in progress. Ruy Ortiz rode up to him, his horse's hooves sending up a crimson spray every few steps.

"Poor sport from this lot, my lord," the Spanish knight said.

"Just as well," Falcon answered, surveying the shambles. "I've a feeling we'll have all the sport we can handle before this journey's over."

Donal crossed the field toward his master, leading two men by halters around their necks. When he was even with Falcon he turned to his charges and said: "My lord wishes some words with you. Answer him well, and he may let you live." The men looked up at Falcon with blank stoicism. Whatever Donal said, they expected no leniency.

"Why were you following us?" Falcon began.

"We heard you had something worth taking," said one.

"Where did you hear this?" Falcon asked.

"Back in our encampment, a few days' ride north of here," said the other.

"Who told you?" Falcon asked.

"I don't know," said one.

"Nor do I," the other concurred.

"Come, gentlemen," Falcon said. "The day is still early, flaying is a tedious process, and it does not end at nightfall. Spare yourselves this and answer me."

"I would like to," said one, "but it was some varlet who came after dark. I couldn't see him clearly. He said that there was a great treasure at an abandoned castle nearby. We thought to take it, but he said it would be easier to take the train that was transporting it. We didn't know whether to believe him, but we kept watch on the place for a few days. When you left with those heavy wagons, we knew that it was true."

"Only half of it," Falcon said. "Not the part about us being easier to take than the castle."

One shrugged philosophically. "One can't be lucky all the time. It seems our luck ran out today."

"It certainly did," Falcon agreed. He nodded to Donal, and the Irishman brained the two bandits with two swift blows of his ax. The second was dead before the first finished his fall.

Bowls of hot gruel were handed out to the men as they returned from the sortie against the bandits. Falcon took his and sat on the back of one of the wagons to eat. It was rough fare, but a soldier on campaign had to be able to live on far less. With two hooked fingers he scooped the bland stuff into his mouth, blowing to cool the scalding porridge.

Simon arrived to give him an account of the takings. The ex-monk was the only man of the whole band besides Falcon who could read and write. He could even do sums to an extent, but only with the old Roman numerals. The Arabic system was only beginning to be adopted in the west.

"We've taken nine mail hauberks of good quality," he reported. "And four pairs of mail hose, twelve good helmets and two helms covering the face, twenty-two shorter shirts of mail of varying quality, thirty-five inferior armors of sundry types, fifty-three swords ranging from good to tolerable, ninety lances or spears, twenty axes, sixteen maces, one hundred five daggers or knives, sixty-two shields of all types, nine bows, two crossbows, together with arrows or quarrels, eighty-three bits, and eleven pairs of spurs, two gilded."

"Load them onto the wagons," Falcon said. "Were the clothes of any worth?"

"A great heap of them, some of good quality but most little better than rags."

"Keep the good stuff, leave the rest," Falcon said.

"Sir, what about the animals? There were twelve good warhorses, and some decent riding or work animals, probably stolen from farms. The rest are spavined or used-up beasts."

"Keep the destriers and the other good beasts," Falcon told him. "We can probably stretch the fodder to accommodate them. Turn the others out. The local peasants will probably find a use for them." Simon bowed and went to do his master's bidding.

"This is a side of battle the poets sing little of." The voice came from above, and Falcon looked up to see Lady Constance looking down at him. She was lying belly-down on a stack of provisions in the wagon, fingers laced and chin resting on fingers. She had discarded her coif and wimple. Her rich chestnut hair flowed free over her back and arms, and she was heartbreakingly beautiful. Falcon had the urge to shove the remains of his gruel in her face.

"Usually it's so glorious," she said. "There are accounts of enemy slain, Saracens cloven to the saddle by paladins, great hosts of foemen routed by a few intrepid knights pure of heart. They never sing of this totting-up of spurs and bits and shirts. It makes you sound more like a merchant than a knight."

"Lady Constance," Falcon said, "my men and I are soldiers. We are not paragons out of some dreamer's fantasy. We fight to live. We do not kill for sport, though many do. Sir Gawain and Roland and the others seem to go through the world adventuring, and their horses never tire or hunger, their armor never rusts, their clothing never rots. We are not so fortunate. All that we have, whether it be arms or apparel or food or animals, needs constant tending, upkeep, or feeding. These bits of armor and equipment we've taken today will keep us in rations and fodder and cloth and leather for several weeks when we're not campaigning."

Taken aback by his vehemence, Constance stuttered: "B-but I did not mean—"

Falcon gave her no chance to recover. He shoved the bowl of gruel under her nose. "You've lived all your life in the courts of the great barons, my lady. You've probably had little call to eat like this, but don't despise it. Some poor devil of a peasant had to work and sweat long hours to grow this grain. It took the craft of a miller to reduce it to cooking condition. What the rats and the insects didn't get is what my men cooked to keep life in their bodies another few hours. None of this comes freely. If men have put their time and labor into a thing, they don't part with it unless they are paid or threatened. We must buy this or steal it. I prefer to buy, although many of my peers think that to loot the peasants is more honorable. For that reason, I keep close account of what we take, even in a little skirmish with bandits such as we had today."

"Sir Draco," she said, "I did not mean to imply—"

Once again, he gave her no time to finish. "Lady, you may bait me as you will at the dinner board, or at the hunt or at a ball in the great hall. The courts are fine places for banter and wordplays and duels of wit. But"—he shoved his face within an inch of her own—"do not try me when I've been killing strangers, even if they were only bandits. A number of those men were knights who had been degraded from their status, lady. Men much like me, in all likelihood. Under slightly different circumstances, I might be lying dead and stripped out there, and one of them escorting you to the bed of your no doubt eager bridegroom. So do not try me further, Lady Constance!" Falcon turned and stormed away.

Constance was stunned by the extraordinary tirade from the usually reticent Sir Draco. She looked up to see Bishop LaCru leaning against another wagon with a faint smile on his lips. "He's not quite your ordinary knight, is he?" the warrior-bishop said.

Constance flushed scarlet. "No! And he's an insufferable boor! I hate him!" She pushed herself back into the cramped living space of her wagon so she would not have to hear LaCru laughing. Suzanne sat by her and poured a cup of red wine for her. The two were forced to sit so close together among the chests and sacks of provisions that they had to interlace their legs in order to fit.

Constance took a drink of the wine and leaned back against a sack of meal. The wagon lurched into motion. "This Falcon," she said, "this knight-errant. He's little more than a brigand himself. He has the manner of a pirate and the instincts of a merchant."

"But he has such a splendid body, my lady!" Suzanne exclaimed. "And he's so handsome! And that man of his, Wulf, why, if I had either of them back here—"

"Suzanne," Constance said, "you're a sweet girl, and I've never had a better maid or traveling companion, but your mind is located about four inches below your navel."

The day wore on. As it wore on, it got colder. Falcon wrapped himself in his heavy cloak and brooded. Wulf rode beside him and kept his peace. When his master was in this mood it was best not to disturb him. When Falcon remembered, it was usually something unpleasant.

The mountainside at Alamut was cold. Draco de Montfalcon hugged a rock in search of shelter from observation by those above. Next to him was his teacher, Osman the Bedouin. They had been making their way up the mountain for two days.

"It's useless," Draco said. "This hill is impregnable."

"It's just a piece of rock," said Osman imperturbably. "And man may climb a rock."

"And at the top of the rock?" Draco demanded. "What's at the top? Assassins, that's what! How are we to deal with them?"

Osman looked up and spread his hands in a plea to Allah for understanding. "My God is witness that this infant has no understanding, nor has he grace nor faith. His perceptions of the world about him proclaim that he is a Frank and not a rational human being." To Moslems, all Westerners were Franks.

Osman glared at Draco, his dark, hawklike desert features as unyielding as those of an Egyptian pharaoh in one of the sculptures that thrust out of the deserts to the south. "What are these Assassins, these Hashishin, but

38

dogs of the Ismaili sect? Have they powers beyond those of other men?"

"Some say they have," Draco said.

"Pah!" Osman spat loudly and dramatically into the abyss below. "How many times have they insulted our master, Suleiman the Wise, with their pathetic attempts upon his life? How many have you seen our master kill in these attempts?"

"Many," Draco acknowledged.

"Now it is time for us to avenge their slights. Our master's honor is not to be treated in such a fashion."

Draco dug his fingers painfully into the rock, searching for any purchase he could find. He had thought this mission insane from the start, and now he believed it to be impossible. He and Osman were making a two-man raid on the most impregnable and terrifying castle in the world: the fortress of Alamut, headquarters of the dread Assassins. They were going to kill the Old Man of the Mountain.

A century before, the sect and the castle had been founded by Hasan-i Sabbāh, the first grand master of the heretical branch of the Ismaili sect commonly called Hashishin because of their use of the drug hashish. The sect had its origins in Egypt, and Hasan had been a supporter of the Fatimid caliphs of Cairo. A change of caliphs had forced the sect to flee to Persia, where they had the support of the Shiite sect which dominated there. Hasan had built the castle at Alamut and added a new doctrine to the already radical beliefs of the Ismaili: The murder of his religious and political enemies was a sacred duty.

Soon the Hashishin were the terror of the Moslem world, with castles from North Africa to Syria, and secret cells in every city. No king, caliph, imam, or magistrate was safe from the daggers of the fanatics.

When the Crusaders arrived, they became victims, too. Their corruption of the name Hashishin gave a new word to the tongues of Europe: Assassin.

In recent years, one of their targets had been Draco's master and teacher, Suleiman the Wise. So far, the attempts had been foiled by Suleiman's uncanny ability to detect the Old Man's minions wherever they lurked in wait for him.

A small clique of Suleiman's soldiers and students had met to decide on an audacious plan. They would go to assassinate the head Assassin. The fortress at Alamut was impregnable to attack, but a small group of men might make their way in undetected. Lots had been drawn, and six had been thus chosen for the mission. Draco was among the six. It was determined that only two could make the final assault, and lots were drawn again. Once more, Draco was one of those chosen.

Now, four men below tended the horses and stood by with medical supplies to be used should the two be wounded in their attempt. Draco and Osman were near the top. Would there be sentries? They had daggers to deal with them if there were any. Then Draco's hand touched the blocks of a cut-stone wall. Osman pulled up beside him, and the two lay gasping in the thin air.

When they were recovered, they assessed their situation, satisfied to find that the wall was not high, and its crenelations were pointed. They had chosen this spot for their ascent betting that the wall atop the supposedly unscalable mountain face would not be formidable.

Osman drew a cord from within his sash. He shook out a wide noose and whirled it a few times, then cast it upward. He missed his first few tries, but finally he looped his noose over one of the pointed crenels. They had chosen the noose because it was silent, unlike the grappling hook. Osman tried his weight on the line, and it held. He cast a final look up. Still no sign of sentries.

Osman began climbing hand over hand. He scaled the wall like a spider until he reached the crenels. With a hand over each of two of the flanking stones, he thrust his head between them for a look up and down the wall. He must have liked what he saw, because Falcon saw him pull himself between the crenels.

Falcon felt a jerk on the line signaling that all was clear, and he began his own ascent. The thin line bit painfully into his palms, for he was far heavier than Osman. Had it not been for the thick calluses of his palms, the line would have cut to bone. As it was, the years of weapon handling, the longer years on the rowing bench, stood him in good stead. He was not able to pass between the crenels. He had to climb over them, and then Osman was pulling him down to crouch on the wall-walk.

He looked up. They had begun their ascent of the final face at first starlight. Now it was near midnight. They had perhaps five more hours of darkness in which to accomplish their mission. How would they find the Old Man in the dark? Somehow, that had never come up in their planning sessions.

The wall seemed to be deserted. Apparently the sect believed its own propaganda and regarded the fortress as truly impregnable. Here and there about the complex of buildings within the walls, small lights could be seen, apparently oil lamps sitting in windows. Once in a while a light would flit between buildings, so at least a few men were still awake and moving about.

Alamut was unlike any true castle of Draco's experience. There was no central keep, and no towers or gate fortifications. Instead, there was a cluster of small stone buildings surrounding one larger one, apparently a mosque. The place looked more like a walled village than a castle.

Osman pointed toward the mosque. "Let's go there," he said. Falcon agreed. It seemed as good a place as any. Stealthily, they made their way along the wall until they found a stair leading to the ground. Their way to the mosque was slow and stumbling through the narrow streets of the little "town." There was one relief: It seemed that there was no livestock sleeping in the streets to be stirred up and make noise.

Eventually, they found themselves a few paces from the mosque, if indeed it was a mosque. There was no minaret, and they could see no pool for ritual ablutions, but that might be explained by the water shortage atop this mountain. They made a circuit of the building. There were narrow slit windows in three of the walls, but no door other than the main entrance. Through the windows, they could vaguely hear the sounds of voices.

There was nothing to do but brazen it out and simply walk in. With the folds of their headdresses drawn across their faces as if against the cold, Draco and Osman entered, their hands gripping the hilts of their daggers beneath their robes. The interior was dim and smoky, illuminated by oil lamps hanging on brass chains from the ceiling.

Inside, they found about fifteen men seated on the floor. Their attention was centered on a man who sat a little apart. He sat crosslegged with a Koran open on a stand before him. The man read from the *suras*, concentrating on those which promised punishment to unbelievers. A man rose from the floor and came to greet Draco and Osman.

"Peace to you," said the greeter.

"And unto you, peace," Draco said, hoping that there was no special response used by the sect.

"You are the brothers from Alexandria?" the man asked.

"Damascus," Osman answered.

"The Old Man will hear your report when he has finished his reading." They found a place to sit, and Draco passed the time by studying the occupants of the room. All were lean, bearded men with fanatical eyes, and they listened to the Old Man read the phrases they had heard a thousand times as if they were hearing them for the first time from the lips of the Prophet himself.

The Old Man appeared to be about thirty years old. The grand master of the sect was always called the Old Man, no matter what his age. This particular Old Man had long black hair hanging in greasy strands over his shoulders and down his back. His beard was long and pointed. His narrow face was dark and ascetic, with eyes like points of fire.

Ceremoniously, the Old Man closed his Koran and sat meditating for a few minutes, during which there was respectful silence in the room. Then he looked up.

"Have any of the brothers reports to make?" he said.

One stood up. "Abdullah ibn Daoud, of the Acre cell," the man said. "Seven of our brothers attacked the grand master of the Hospitalers and his officers as they emerged from their church. The grand master was but wounded, but four of his high-ranking officers were slain. All of the brothers died gloriously."

The Old Man raised his hands piously. "Even now, they enjoy the delights of Paradise," he intoned. The others made ritual responses.

"Two brothers from the Damascus cell are here, master," said the man who had greeted Draco and Osman.

The two stood and approached the Old Man. "We have come to report on the latest attempt to kill Suleiman the Wise," Osman said.

"Good," said the Old Man. "How did it go?"

"It failed," Osman said, drawing his dagger. "Now, die, Ismaili dog!" And he and Draco fell upon the Old Man, stabbing furiously.

FOUR

The villagers gaped at the armed men as the train filed into the little town. Falcon surveyed the place. It was no different from thousands of others: a huddle of mud-and-timber houses surrounding a small church. The people were the same ragged peasants who occupied every other village. Perhaps they were a bit more villainous-looking than most, but that might be the result of the treasure he was escorting. Lately, the faces of many he saw took on a thievish look. Even some of his own men were beginning to look extremely untrustworthy.

A priest in a threadbare robe came to greet them. He walked up to the group of horsemen that included Falcon, LaCru, Ruy Ortiz, and Rudolph of Austria. Not sure which was the leader, the priest addressed a spot somewhere over their heads.

"Welcome to our poor village, gentlemen. If you are here to loot our town, I ask that you refrain from burning our houses, now that winter is upon us."

"We are just passing through," Falcon said patiently. He had had to make this speech many times before. Villagers always assumed that an unfamiliar army was there to loot and burn. "What we take, we'll pay for. Tell your parishioners they can bring their livestock back from the woods now. We've been on the road for days and we're starved for fresh meat. We'll be staying here for the night."

"Doubly welcome, then," said the priest. "With so many soldiers here, we can sleep safe tonight."

"The outlaws have been robbing you, then?" asked Bishop LaCru.

"Not just outlaws, my lord," the priest said. In armor, with his featureless shield, LaCru gave no indication of being a bishop.

"Who, then?" Falcon asked.

"Why," the priest said, "Fulk the Devil, of course."

The knights and the bishop looked at one another in puzzlement. Falcon dismounted and handed his reins to Wulf. The others dismounted likewise.

"First we eat," Falcon said. "Then, good father, you must tell us about Fulk the Devil."

Fulk sat gnawing a hambone, elbows resting on a table of rough-hewn planks. The table was littered with bones, crusts, and fruit peels from former meals. A wooden tankard of ale slowly leaked from a crack in one side, forming a small puddle on the table. A rat appeared from beneath the straw heaped in a corner of the room, and Fulk snatched up an old beef bone and threw it with great accuracy, smashing the rodent against a wall, where it squealed for a moment, then stiffened and died.

"Hah! Got you, you little bastard!" Fulk cried. Fulk's mountain castle overlooked the only passable road through this part of the mountains. The room in which he now sat was littered with the loot he had gathered from passing merchants. Besides the stolen goods, there were sacks of coins from the ransoms he had taken. He had his pick of the prettiest peasant girls of the district, whom he collected by the simple expedient of sending his men to snatch the girls and kill any menfolk who dared to interfere. Life was good in Fulk's castle.

A man called from outside the doorway: "My lord!"

"What is it, Pierre?" Fulk asked, setting down the ham and taking up his tankard.

"A man here to see you."

"To see me?" Fulk said, dumbfounded. Nobody had sought Fulk out in many years. Quite the contrary, in fact. "Bring the wretch in, then," Fulk commanded.

Pierre came in, shoving a trembling man before him. Well might he tremble. Pierre had had his nose and both ears removed by the public executioner for some past indiscretion. A hairlip made him no prettier, exposing teeth and gum all the way up into where his right nostril should have been. Some skin disease caused his hair to grow in widely scattered patches.

"What do you want?" Fulk demanded.

"My lord," the trembling wretch said, "I have come to tell you how you may grow rich beyond your wildest dreams."

"What did he have?" Fulk asked Pierre.

"Just this," Pierre said, tossing a clinking bag onto the table. Fulk picked it up and poked through it with a filthy finger. "Was this all?"

"He was riding a good rounsey," Pierre said. "It's in the stables now."

"Now, varlet," Fulk said, leveling his bloodshot gaze on the shrinking figure before him, "tell me: Was this all you had when you rode in here? If you're afraid of Pierre, remember who's lord here and why. He's as pretty and meek as a maid compared to me."

The man looked back and forth between the two daunting men. At last, he said: "Lord, there was a gold ring, set with an amethyst—"

47

Fulk held out his hand, palm up, to Pierre. "Give it to me, you shit-eating vulture, before I cut your balls off."

Pierre reached into his codpiece and took out the ring. He dropped it into Fulk's palm. Fulk examined it as he picked his nose.

"Well," Fulk said at length, "you've made me a little richer already. Sit down and tell me how I may become richer still." The man seated himself at a bench across the table from Fulk. "Pierre," Fulk said, "send up a wench with more ale." Pierre left.

"Lord, I am Jean the Chamberlain. My master, who must remain nameless, wishes you to know that a train of men, escorting a great treasure, will soon be passing through your domain."

"Treasure?" Fulk said. "Why does this nameless master of yours wish to inform me of this?"

"Let us say," Jean stated, "that he has reasons for wanting the treasure in any hands other than those which now hold it."

"And what is the nature of this treasure?" Fulk asked.

"I do not know. Only a few men do, but it is said to be fabulous, greater than anything seen in this generation."

Fulk's eyes gleamed with greed. "What is the nature of this escort?" The ale arrived, delivered by a buxom peasant girl with a pitcher in each hand. She refilled Fulk's leaky vessel, then poured a cup for Jean. The chamberlain grasped the cup in both shaky hands and poured the ale down his parched throat.

"There are two hundred men, lord," Jean said.

"Two hundred," Fulk mused. "That's nearly as many as I have." Fulk cared little for the idea of an even fight.

"Only a few are knights," Jean said. "Some are mount-ed men-at-arms, others are common footmen, although

48

all will be mounted. Their progress will be very slow, because of the mountain roads and the heavy wagons."

"Heavy wagons, eh?" Fulk chuckled. He grabbed the peasant girl and held her to him, his big paw idly going up and down her thigh beneath her patched dress. She bore his ministrations stoically. "How soon will they be here?"

"Within two days," Jean said. "I have been riding ahead of them."

"Good, good. Now, how much ransom will your master pay for you?"

Jean turned even paler. "Ransom? But I may have made you the richest baron in France! Surely you would not hold me for whatever paltry ransom my master might pay?"

"And why not?" Fulk asked. "I haven't been successful by letting prey slide through my grasp. This treasure may exist, or it may not. I may take it, or I may fail. But I have you right here. How much?"

"Very little, I fear," Jean said, sweating heavily.

"Pierre!" Fulk shouted. The fearsome man-at-arms entered. "Take him out and cut his throat. Toss his carcass into the gully downwind." Pierre took the chamberlain by the shoulder.

"Wait!" Jean squealed. "Let me send word to my master! It may be that he values my services more highly than I have thought."

"That's better," Fulk said. "Take him to the kennel and chain him up with the others."

Pierre took Jean away, and Fulk rose to his feet. He picked up the serving girl and threw her to her back on the table. Tossing her skirts up over her waist, he began fumbling with his hose.

Falcon carved slices of the roasted mutton with his

curved Saracen dagger. He laid the meat on a thick slab of dark peasant bread he held in one hand. Seating himself on a chest and leaning back against a wagon wheel, he bit off a huge mouthful of meat and bread and chewed it ecstatically. Ordinarily, mutton was considered to be too coarse and strong to be correct food for the nobility. Beef, pork, and especially wild game were all proper fare for persons of good breeding. Nonetheless, Falcon reflected, there was nothing like rich mutton, sizzling hot and dripping with fat, to warm the innards when traveling on a cold winter night. He washed down the rather dry, bulky food with wine, mulled with spices over a fire. Soon he felt a comfortable, mellow glow and decided that this mission might not turn out so badly after all. Then he remembered Fulk the Devil.

The wagon he was leaning against was the one Constance and Suzanne were traveling in. From time to time, a bone came flying out the back of the wagon, to land in the withered brown grass of the common, where it was pursued by the village curs. Eventually, Constance emerged from the wagon, licking her fingers. Her chin was shiny with grease.

"God, that was good!" she said. "I'll never disdain peasant food again. I was so hungry I thought I'd die waiting for that sheep to cook. Sir Draco, might I trouble you for some of that wine?"

Falcon handed her the steaming pitcher, and she reached into her wagon and withdrew a cup. She poured and drank the hot, spicy beverage gratefully. She then sat on the ground facing Falcon.

"Sir Draco," Constance asked, "who is this Fulk the Devil everybody is babbling about?"

"What you would expect," Falcon answered. "A murderous swine with a band of unhung cutthroats at his command. He has some pretensions to noble blood and supposedly owes fealty to John of England, but that just means he's his own master for the time being. He plunders the countryside and any traffic that comes through, and his men can seize any pretty girls they please."

"How can people of good blood do such things?" Constance demanded.

Falcon looked at her pityingly. "My lady, I've know a great many men like Fulk. I've never encountered one like those stainless knights you hear about in the poems. For most of the nobility of Christendom, good blood is an excuse to shed any that isn't."

"Whereas pay is your excuse," Constance said. Falcon sighed. For nearly three minutes, they had been having a civil conversation. He might have known that it could not last.

"Lady, my men and I serve for pay as others serve for fealty. As often as not, we serve some lout little better than this Fulk who hires us to plunder some other bandit. It's paltry, but it keeps us fed. We don't burn villages or rob peasants, but neither will we be peasants ourselves. Soldiers without wars can starve just as do peasants when the crops fail."

"Then, for the sake of your welfare, we must pray that the supply of wars does not dry up," Constance said acidly.

"Little chance of that," Falcon said. He could not remember the last time a woman had infuriated him so. With men it was so much simpler. You could always kill a man who insulted you.

Wulf sat at a fire, picking the last bits of succulent flesh from the rack of sheep ribs. As he cleaned each rib, he tossed it to a pack of village dogs and watched with amusement as they fought over it. A man had to find his entertainment wherever he could on a trip like this. There were no harpers or jugglers hereabout, and Falcon had expressly forbidden the men to have anything to do with the village women, in the interests of discipline and good relations. Then he remembered Suzanne.

Casually, Wulf stood, wiping his greasy fingers on his mailshirt to prevent rust. "I'll go check the sentries," he said. The others seated about the campfire didn't even look up.

Wulf made his way through the dimness to the wagon Suzanne shared with her lady. On the other side of the wagon, he could hear Falcon and Lady Constance engaged in one of their usual acrimonious conversations. Odd, he thought. His lord usually had such a way with the ladies. Unfortunate, for they made a handsome couple. It was to his advantage, though, because the argument would keep them from hearing him.

Silently, he crept behind the wagon, staying out of their line of vision. He climbed onto the tail and parted the curtains. The inside was veiled in obscurity. "Suzanne?" he whispered.

Hands reached out and tugged him inside. "It's Wulf, isn't it?" Her lips were so close to his ear that he felt the warmth of her breath.

"Yes," he said. He could feel her shifting and he heard sounds of rustling cloth. Then he felt her hands pulling at his own clothes. It was not easy to get the mailshirt off in the confined space, but her urgency would brook no delays. When he was suitably stripped, Suzanne pulled him to her violently.

"We'll have to be quick," she said. "They'll be yelled out soon."

Constance glared at Falcon, and he glared back. For several minutes, neither had been able to think of anything suitably cutting to say, and now they contented themselves with rancorous silence. Soon, both found their hostile meditations distracted by some strange sounds coming from within the wagon: muffled gaspings and moanings. The wagon itself was beginning to rock and creak.

"What's going on in there?" demanded Constance.

"I'm afraid to look," Falcon said.

"I'm not." She stood and strode to the back of the wagon, and Falcon accompanied her. He peered over her shoulder as she drew the curtain aside. They were greeted by the sight of the moonlight reflecting from a pair of pale buttocks in violent motion. Just above the buttocks a pair of feet were crossed, their toes curled tightly under. Even in the dim light they could see that the bare fundament was covered with thin, crisscrossed scars.

Constance dropped the curtain. She said, very slowly so that Falcon would not detect her mortification, "Those feet belong to my maid, Suzanne."

Falcon was not fooled. Even in the moonlight he could see that she had gone as dark as a Saracen. In daylight her color would have been crimson. "The backside, I fear, belongs to my man Wulf. I'd know it anywhere."

"Do you know all your men by their buttocks?" she asked sweetly.

"Just him," Falcon answered, willing himself not to crack a smile.

"I trust your familiarity involves no activities punishable by death."

Falcon ignored the jibe. "Did you notice all those scars?"

"I did," Constance admitted. "He must have been a runaway serf."

"I look much the same," Falcon said. "We're both striped like that from neck to heel."

"Oh," Constance said, intrigued but unwilling to show it. "Were you a runaway serf, too?"

"No," Falcon said. "We both spent two years rowing a Turkish galley." He turned and walked back to resume his seat. The hook was in now and he wouldn't even have to pull her in. He poured himself another cup of wine.

Constance fought with her curiosity for a full minute, then gave in. She sat beside Falcon and held her cup out to be refilled. Everyone else except the sentries had bedded down for the night, and the only sounds were the groans coming from inside the wagon, which they ignored.

"You were captured in the Crusade?" Constance asked at length.

"After Hattin," Falcon answered.

"Hattin!" Constance exclaimed. It had been the greatest battle of the Crusade, and it had been a disaster for the Christians. "You must have been boys!"

"We were young," Falcon admitted. "We were captured at an oasis after the battle and marched to the coast. There we were sold aboard a ship called the *Sultana*, captained by one Rustam the Magnanimous, as vicious a pirate as ever drew breath. His slave master was named Abu. He had a taste for the whip and for young men. I killed him when the ship was captured by the caliph's pirate catchers."

"And then?" she asked, now totally enthralled.

"The commander of the ship that took the *Sultana* was Suleiman the Wise, a famous teacher and magistrate. He freed Wulf and me and took us into his service."

"You served a pagan?" she said, aghast. "After they took you prisoner and sold you onto that galley?"

54

"I wasn't taken by Saracens," he said. "It was a renegade German knight named Gunther Valdemar."

"A Christian!" she said, profoundly shocked.

"I have my doubts about that," Falcon commented. "A couple of years ago I caught up with Valdemar and killed him. He tricked me into finishing him too quickly." His face was grim now, and Constance shuddered inwardly. She knew she wasn't getting the whole story on this man Valdemar.

"In any case," Falcon continued, now affecting a light tone, "that's how I came to know Wulf by his striped rump."

The wagon was now silent, and Falcon heard Wulf tiptoeing away. "It's time for me to check the sentries and get some sleep, my lady," Falcon said, lurching to his feet. For the first time in their relationship, she didn't try to come up with a barbed remark to part on.

As Constance climbed into the wagon, Suzanne was tugging her dress down over her plump thighs. The smell that assailed her as she entered was earthy, feral, and strangely exciting.

"It smells like a stable in here!" Constance leaned over and slapped Suzanne twice across the face, as hard as she could. "You disobedient bitch! How could you fornicate in here with the Saxon churl while I sat with his master outside? You sounded like wild boars fighting in a mudhole!"

"I'm sorry, my lady," the girl sobbed, hiding her face behind her crossed arms. "I couldn't help it!" Both her tears and her humility were patently false.

"I should flog you within an inch of your life!" Constance sat fuming for a minute or two, then, for the second time that night, her curiosity got the better of her. She sat next to Suzanne and leaned close. "Now, tell me," she said, eagerly, "how was it?"

Falcon was annoyed at the silly grin Wulf wore all the next day. Once he kicked the Saxon in the rump on general principles. "There will be no more wallowing in that girl on this mission," Falcon commanded sternly.

"As you command, my lord," Wulf said, still grinning. Falcon glared at Wulf as the Saxon rode away. Why should he have all the fun?

The village was well behind them now, and they were deep into the territory controlled by Fulk the Devil. Falcon wondered whether the bandit rated the appellation. Every petty robber baron with a reputation for exceptional brutality was always known locally as "the Devil," "the Wolf," "the Strong," or some such. They were a poisonous breed, and Christendom was full of them.

Under strong kings who stayed at home and administered their domains, such highborn banditry withered. But now, with weaklings and fools predominating upon European thrones, and with the best of the nobility off crusading, armored thieves and their castles were everywhere. They extorted wealth from any merchant passing through their territory, robbed peasant and church with impartiality, and gleefully tortured anyone suspected of hiding the slightest item of value.

There was, as far as Falcon could judge, a single bright spot in this familiar, dreary scene: The robber barons were predators who preyed upon the weak. More precisely, they were not predators at all, but scavengers who would never risk an even fight. Falcon was a true predator. Fulk the Devil, by comparison, was a carrion crow. Falcon, true to his name, was a genuine bird of prey.

Then he reflected that any creature with teeth or claws will attack if desperate enough or tempted strongly enough. The treasure he was escorting, whatever it was, might be the temptation that could make this particular crow think he was an eagle.

The carrion bird in question was at that moment observing the progress of Falcon's convoy from a crag of rock overlooking the road which he regarded as his own. Beside him was the hideous Pierre. They looked grim at the prospect of the men passing below. They knew hard-bitten professional soldiers when they saw them, and these were well mounted and armed to the teeth.

"I see no rabble down there," Fulk commented. "That lying chamberlain said that most would be mere armed varlets. We'll impale him on a red-hot spike as soon as we get back." The thought cheered him. It was one of his favorite methods of dealing with those who displeased him.

"Maybe they're not as tough as they look," said Pierre, with little conviction. Then the wagons came into view, and the two studied them closely. The wagons were small, but very stoutly made, and they creaked and groaned along as if they bore the weight of all the world's sins. The eyes of both men lit up at the sight.

"It must be gold to weigh so much!" Fulk exulted.

"How much do you think it is?" asked Pierre eagerly.

Fulk's mind made a dim attempt to calculate the capacity of the wagon beds, but he got bogged down in trying to think in terms of bushel baskets or wine kegs. "A lot," he said at last. "More than we or all our ancestors have ever seen, I'll warrant." Both men actually began to drool.

"There's another wagon," said Pierre. Fulk glanced at it, but it was clear that it carried no treasure, for it did not move as if heavy-laden.

"Probably just provisions or fodder for the animals," Fulk said.

"Then why are so many men guarding it?" Pierre asked.

Fulk looked closer. There did seem to be an unusual number of men riding near the wagon, and a crossbowman was riding on top. A man in glittering mail rode up near to the back of the wagon and leaned forward as if to talk to someone on the other side of the rear curtains.

"There's someone in there," Fulk said. "Didn't that chamberlain say there was a noble lady riding with them?"

"Some viscount's daughter or niece, I think," Pierre answered.

"Worth a good ransom, then," Fulk observed.

"Why bother if we can take a treasure like that?" Pierre protested.

"A man can always use a little more loot," Fulk said. "In any case, I grow weary of the company of lowborn scum like you and the rest. It's time I enjoyed the companionship of my own kind for a change." He mused for a while, scratching the lice on his scalp. "Besides, I haven't had anything but peasant bedding for years."

FIVE

Falcon was riding at the head of the column when the Welshmen came riding back from their scouting mission ahead of the main body. They reigned in beside him, and Rhys gave their report.

"Castle up ahead about a mile. It sits on a crag about six bowshots above the road. There's a narrow road leading up to it, and it's very steep."

"Any sign of men on the battlements or on the road?" Falcon asked.

"Not even a flag fluttering," the Welshman answered. "Plenty of sign about, though. Tracks and fresh horse turds everywhere."

"What's our road like below the castle?" Falcon demanded.

"Narrow. The uphill slope is covered with big boulders you could hide an army behind."

"They'll probably ambush us there, then, if they've the nerve," Falcon said.

"Surely they won't be mad enough to try," protested Bishop LaCru, who rode with Falcon.

"They might," Falcon said. He looked up at the clouds that hung low overhead. "There's snow in those clouds. I'd hoped to get out of these mountains before the first snow struck. What a time to be confronted with a fight." Falcon fumed silently for a while. Ordinarily, he would have stepped up the pace and gone past the castle as quickly as possible. As it was, he was constrained by the damned wagons to this snail's pace. He detested the thought of being stopped by a snowstorm within reach of the robber's castle. To have to set up camp on the narrow road while in marching order instead of in a defended campsite was intolerable. They could fall prey to a band smaller than their own.

Falcon called Wulf to his side. "Have the column close up," Falcon ordered. "From here on, we travel close. Front and rear guard will do us no good here. Have every man keep his eyes peeled for attack from the front and from upslope."

"If this Fulk knows these mountain trails," LaCru pointed out, "they may be able to get behind us."

"It's possible," Falcon admitted. "Nothing much we can do except watch for it, though." That was the worst part of their situation. Falcon, without undue modesty, considered himself to be the best tactician in Christendom. He had to be. With an army so small, the only way he could hope to prevail was through outmaneuvering his enemy. On this narrow road, compelled to protect the wagons, there was no scope for maneuver or mobility.

He had built this little army, the first of its kind, in order to institute a new kind of warfare, fought by a new kind of warrior. Before the Crusades, all military service had been a matter of feudal obligation. A lord would grant a knight land and serfs sufficient to support himself, his family, and his horse. In return, the knight owed his lord forty days' military service each year. The rest of the time was taken up in tending his estate, and in any case the campaigning season was short because the all-important horses had to have sufficient grass. Men fought from May to August, then they went home, if they lived.

This had been adequate when wars had consisted mainly of raiding the nearest neighbor. In those days war was a summer's work for a man of good blood, and the occasional call to repel Moors or Magyars or Vikings had added the prospect of an exhilarating outing. The Moors and Magyars and Vikings were long departed from the plains and coasts of Christendom, though, and warfare had settled into desultory raiding and besieging of petty castles. The last great leader of a national army had been Charlemagne, and he'd been dead for nearly three centuries when an unprecedented event had stirred up the ancient stagnation of Europe. The Pope had preached a Crusade, and Europe was on the move.

Part military exercise, part religious pilgrimage, part looting expedition, the Crusade had changed military thought. Campaigns could last for years, and forty days' service was not enough. A knight's lord might depart for home before the knight was ready to leave the Holy Land, or he might be killed, leaving the knight at loose ends. The result was a chaotic system of temporary fealties, the establishment of military-monastic orders such as the Templars, and, more and more often, service for pay. Gradually, true professional armies had grown up in Palestine.

Into this ferment, twenty years before, had come the very young Draco de Montfalcon. His years in Palestine had contained first unbelievable brutalities, and then education in a culture so refined that Europe was a sink of barbarism by comparison. He had learned well. On his return to Europe, his name changed to Falcon, he had set about building a type of army not seen in Europe since the collapse of the Western Roman Empire seven hundred years before.

He wanted no mob of undisciplined knights, no rabble of untrained footmen, and no straggling tail of camp followers. He chose knights who were willing to accept discipline and men-at-arms who were outstanding experts with whatever weapons or skills they possessed, regardless of their birth. He kept the whole force mounted for mobility, even those who ordinarily fought on foot. The men swore an oath to him, but they served him for pay and for whatever loot he could bring their way. He hired their services to the highest bidder, and they had always been successful. His reputation was beginning to spread.

There were, of course, difficulties. Pay was one of them. Europe's economy was based largely on barter, and there was always a shortage of coined money. When coinage was available it was usually debased, clipped, or broken to such an extent that the only way to determine its value was to guess at its alloy and weigh it as bulk metal. Only the cities of Italy produced good coins of reliable value. Soldiers could not be paid in livestock or bulk goods if they were to be expected to march anywhere at their captain's order. Finding money to pay his troops was one of Falcon's continuing headaches.

After the years of hard training, of perfecting his men in the arts of maneuver on the field in obedience to his command, he was confident of his army's ability to outmatch an enemy of far greater numbers. Now, he was galled at the thought that his splendid professional force was in danger from the scum led by a human jackal like Fulk the Devil.

As Falcon brooded thus, the first flakes of snow began to blow into his face.

* * *

Fulk studied the men assembled in the small courtyard of his castle. Even by the standards of a brutal age, Fulk's followers were filthy, vicious, and depraved. Nearly every one of them had cropped ears or nose, branded brow or cheek, scars from manacles around wrist, ankle, and neck, or other marks of society's disfavor. Among them they had committed every crime conceivable to the mind of man, and they were eager to commit more. They knew that their lives were destined to end on the gallows, the wheel, the rack, or some other place for the imaginative disposal of felons, but these men feared little except hard labor. Fulk was deeply satisfied with them. They would happily perpetrate any horror he ordered them to, and in return he would be more than pleased to sacrifice every one of them for any profit or advantage. That was the best thing about them: They were so eminently replaceable.

"Now listen, you filth," began Fulk in his jovial fashion, "this is an especially fine prize we're after, so anyone who fails in his duty will be dealt with harshly. If any one of you fails me today, I won't just nail a red-hot spike through his belly the way I usually do. I'll think of something really cruel. You all know what to do—you've done this often enough before. Above all, I want those wagons. I also want that lady. Except for purposes of hauling her up here, you're to keep your paws off her. A viscount's kinswoman's not for the likes of you. Otherwise, you're free to mount anything you can capture, but wait till you're back here to do it.

"Are you ready?" The men made a sort of collective growl signifying assent and enthusiasm. "Then arm yourselves and take your places." The men began pulling on their shirts of mail or iron scales and their helmets, and they buckled on swords and hefted axes and pole-arms. The years of robbery had provided even the lowest of them with adequate armor and weapons. Fulk went into his chamber to arm himself.

He threw open his arms chest, and Pierre helped him on with his gear. Over his filthy everyday clothes Fulk pulled on a gambeson. This was a long coat of stout leather quilted with a stuffing of horsehair. Here and there it was pierced with holes for ventilation. Pierre picked up the rolled-up hauberk of mail, and Fulk thrust his hands through the armholes and raised the mass of iron over his head. It slid down his arms to his shoulders and unrolled of its own weight with Pierre helping to straighten out folds or kinks that might cause it to hang up. Fully unrolled, the hauberk fell to Fulk's knees. Its sleeves stopped at the elbows and were roomy. Tight sleeves to the wrist were now the fashion, but Fulk still preferred the old style.

Fulk took a handful of the mail in each fist and tugged the skirts up a few inches. Pierre pulled Fulk's swordbelt tight around his wasit, and Fulk released the mail so that a fold hung over his belt. This transferred the weight of the long skirts to his waist instead of forcing his shoulders to bear the entire weight. The hauberk weighed perhaps fifty pounds, but Fulk, like all knights, had trained in armor every day from early youth and was scarcely aware of the weight.

He drew his sword and glanced along its well-polished length. The edge was keen, and the notches from its last few fights had been filed and honed away. The sword was long and heavy, undecorated and functional. Satisfied that his sword was in order, he sheathed it. A heavy dagger with a fifteen-inch blade hung on the side opposite the sword. Fulk pulled the mail coif up over his head and adjusted its padding for comfort, then tied its lace. He picked up a round-topped helmet with a nasal and clapped it over the coif.

He mounted his horse in the courtyard, and one of the men handed his shield up to him. It was long and triangular, and it was curved to improve balance and give protection to the sides. He had never gotten around to adopting an identifying device, so the shield's face was painted plain red. He looked up and smiled at the falling snow. So much the better.

"I hate this," Falcon said, peering into the snow ahead. "An army in marching order is all flank. There's too much to protect and no depth of defense."

Bishop LaCru didn't answer. The point was too obvious for comment. He hefted his heavy cudgel and muttered a string of prayers, not from fear, but from long habit as a calming exercise. He'd served God, king, and Pope well. He had fought on Crusade, and if he died today he was sure of his salvation. That was the important thing. Even for a high churchman, life was not so good that it was something worth hanging on to at all costs. He was as near to being fearless as a sane and reasonable man could be.

"There's the castle," Falcon said quietly. They studied it as they approached. It was dimly visible through the falling snow: a simple tower jutting from a crag of rock with a low-walled enclosure below it. It was as crude and primitive as a fortress could be and still rate the name of castle, but it served its purpose. Its high position obviated the necessity of a moat or high walls, and it completely dominated this stretch of road. As a robber's lair, it couldn't have been improved upon.

"Everyone be ready," shouted Falcon, unnecessarily. Everyone had been fully ready for hours. The archers and crossbowmen scanned the slopes as far as the range limits of their weapons, and the others fingered the grips and shafts of their arms. There was a hundredth testing of shield straps and helmet cords and the inevitable half-nervous, half-eager waiting for action.

"There they are!" Wulf called. As they rounded a bend almost directly below the castle, they caught sight of a band of mounted men a hundred yards ahead. There were about twenty of them, bunched onto a wide spot on the road. It would have been an easy matter to charge and ride them down, but there were the wagons to consider. They were certainly the principal target.

"A diversion, Sir Draco?" queried LaCru.

"Certainly. The real attack will come from upslope or from behind. We proceed at our present pace." They plodded forward. The strange horsemen stood their ground. There was no hail or challenge. Some of them couched lances, the others held axes or bared swords.

Without signal, the lancers charged. At the same instant, a hail of missiles rained down from the crags above. Stones and javelins and a few arrows cascaded against uplifted shields or clanged from helmets. Falcon's men wheeled their mounts to face the slope.

Falcon did not charge to meet the oncoming horsemen, but instead sat his mount and awaited them, shield at the ready and ax in his hand. The foremost horseman bore down upon him with lance aimed straight at Falcon's throat. A second before the point would have struck, Falcon leaned aside and raised his shield six inches. As he stood in his stirrups, the lance shaft brushed his left shoulder. His ax came crashing down to split the man's helmet like a melon. As the corpse rode past, the ax broke loose with a squelching sound. Then two more were on him, hewing with their swords. The one on Falcon's right raised his sword to strike, and Falcon sank his ax into the man's unshielded thigh. With a shriek, the man tumbled beneath the hooves of the milling horses. Then Falcon was dizzied by a blow to his head from the left. The other horseman had tried to take advantage of his engagement with his late adversary, but Falcon's superb Saracen helmet caused the blade to glance harmlessly away. He turned to deal with the man, but at that instant Bishop LaCru's great bludgeon smashed the man's helmet from behind. Blood gushed from his mouth and nose and his eyes started from their sockets as he hurtled to the ground.

"You bloodied that one, bishop!" Falcon shouted. "You'll have to do penance, now!"

"I must be more careful," LaCru said. He grinned ferociously. Even a lifetime in holy orders couldn't still the bloodlust of a French noble.

Then they heard cries of dismay behind them. Falcon's men were frantically trying to turn their horses as a dense pack of horsemen and foot soldiers came charging up from *below*.

"My God!" Falcon said, bewildered for the first time in years. "The buggers are charging from downslope!" It was a totally unexpected tactical maneuver. Armored horsemen *always* charged downhill where they could, to build up smashing momentum to destroy the enemy line. In a flash, he saw how well planned this ambush was. There was no need for a smashing charge, because the treasure train was strung out in a thin line. All that was necessary was to get a mass of men against the part of the column where the wagons were. The rest of the escort would be of little defensive use because of the narrowness of the road. Falcon cursed himself in lurid terms for underestimating Fulk.

"The wagons!" Falcon shouted. "Everyone back to the wagons and defend them!"

"How?" LaCru demanded, pointing. The road was a chaos of screaming, kicking horses and mounted and dismounted men struggling fiercely to kill or to live. There was not an inch of space for a man on horseback to force his way back to the wagons.

Falcon didn't hesitate. He leaped from his saddle and scrambled up the slope for a few yards, then began making his way back down his line. He could see that his men were handling the raiders without too much difficulty. That was to be expected. Fulk's scum weren't in the same class with Falcon's finely trained men. Still, it was rough going. Wulf, as usual, followed a few steps behind his lord, watching for rear and flank attack. A ragged bandit in a scale shirt attacked, and Falcon axed him down almost absentmindedly. Then he saw the heaviest of the fighting going on around the wagons. The crossbowmen and the two Welshmen were standing atop the wagons, calmly shooting into the struggling mass below, killing a man with every shot. Men and horses were so tangled that some were being suffocated, and their feet and hooves were churning the road to bloody mush. The falling snow laid an incongruously cheerful pall over it all.

Falcon and Wulf began hewing their way in toward the wagons. This was easy, because the bandits had their attention on the defenders around the wagons and they could simply chop them down from behind. Rupert Foul-Mouth stood on the driver's seat of the foremost wagon, laying about him with a huge wooden maul—a hammer intended primarily for driving stakes but equally good for crushing skulls.

On other wagons he could see his knights directing the action as best they could. Ruy Ortiz and Rudolph of Austria had their horses backed against the wagons and were chopping away with their long swords. Beside one wagon Sir Andrew the Scot was fighting dismounted. Sir Andrew fought with a long-handled poleax which featured a combination ax, hook, and spearhead. He called the vicious thing Maid's Kiss, and he was uncommonly deadly with it. The concentration of the fighting here made the ground exceedingly treacherous with its litter of bodies, weapons, and spare limbs, and the mush of mud, blood, and snow.

Falcon fought his way to Rupert's wagon and hauled himself up. "Ah, there y'are, my lord," Rupert said. He felled a bandit with a shattering blow of his maul. "Eat that, ye lizard-fucking toad!" He turned back toward Falcon. "I feared the bastards had pulled you down. I reckon all's in hand here."

It was clear that the robbers were losing heart. Even in their unfavorable position, Falcon's men were making a dreadful hash of the undisciplined rabble opposing them. The element of surprise had not been sufficient to shake the confidence and discipline of Falcon's professional soldiers. As Falcon watched, Rudolph's sword, Cheeseparer, lopped a final head, then the bandits were falling back, retreating up the road to their castle.

Up on the road, Falcon could see a big man, mounted and in full armor, waving his fist and cursing, trying to drive the men back down to take the wagons. It was to no avail. They had had enough. That, Falcon thought, must be Fulk the Devil. From this distance, he was as anonymous as any other armored man.

The noise and shouting began to die away, and Falcon climbed down from the wagon to check the damage. His men were already efficiently stripping the bodies. The wounded men were being cared for. The wounded from Falcon's band, at any rate. Any of the bandits still living were summarily finished off. The air was full of groans, and the snow was covering the blood.

"Wagons all secure, my lord," Ortiz reported. "They didn't take a one of them."

"Good," Falcon said. "What about Lady Constance?"

He noted that her wagon had become somewhat separated from the others.

"The lady?" said Rudolph, wiping the blood and brains from Cheeseparer. "Forgot all about her. I think everyone was anxious to preserve the treasure." He seemed unconcerned. There was no shortage of noble ladies.

"Damn!" Falcon sprinted to where the women's wagon sat, slightly askew. Its oxen blinked about them as if wondering what all the excitement was about. "Constance!" Falcon jerked the curtain aside. There was nobody inside. "Everybody up and search for Lady Constance!" Falcon shouted. "She may have tried to hide someplace."

Wulf came running up. "Suzanne?" he asked.

"She's gone, too," Falcon answered.

The men searched, but the two women were nowhere to be found.

Constance and Suzanne huddled in the bed of their wagon, terrified by the frightening din from outside. Once, Constance had looked out through the curtain to a hellish scene of men shouting and hacking at one another in a bestial fury. No woman of her class could be entirely unacquainted with warfare, but she had never seen the action so close before. Even as she withdrew, she was spattered with droplets of blood.

"Who is winning, my lady?" asked Suzanne. The girl was trembling with fright, but she gripped a dagger and had every intention of using it if necessary.

"Who can tell?" Constance said. "They're fighting like beasts out there, only beasts quit when they're hurt. Those men seem determined to die."

Suddenly, the curtain was jerked aside and a man thrust head and shoulders into the wagon. Both women screamed. The man looked like a demon come straight from hell to fetch them away. The face within the iron mail coif had no nose, just a gaping, triangular hole like a skull's, and a grotesque harelip exposed twisted yellow fangs.

Suzanne recovered first and thrust at the hideous face with her dagger. The man blocked the blade casually with a mailed forearm and backhanded the girl, knocking her unconscious. Chuckling, he wrapped an arm around Constance's waist and plucked her lightly from the wagon. His foul, winy breath washed over her face and turned her stomach. "Got the bitch!" he shouted to his cohorts outside. Constance tried to fight, but the man was swathed in iron and there was no place to hit or bite him. The only possible target for her teeth would have been his nose, but somebody had already deprived her of that objective.

"How do you know that's the one?" said another bandit. The noseless one glanced back inside at Suzanne.

"This one's clothes are better," he said. "But bring the other along in case. Another wench will always come in handy." The other bandit scrambled into the wagon and emerged with Suzanne slung over his shoulder like a sack of grain. "Hurry up," the noseless one urged. "The fighting's coming back this way."

Constance found herself thrown face down over a saddle, and the pommel jammed into her belly so sharply that she thought it would come out through her backbone. Her nose was filled with the smell of the sweat-soaked horse blanket, but at least it was preferable to the noseless one's breath. She tried to calm herself. She was a lady of good birth, so she would be held for ransom. If Falcon wasn't killed, he would try to rescue her. Or would he? He didn't seem to be terribly chivalrous. Then she was distracted by a new agony as the horse set off at a trot, each step ramming the pommel into her until all she could feel was a ball of flame from her hips to her sternum.

The ride to the castle seemed endless. Maybe the man really was a demon, and she was being taken to hell. She couldn't remember having done anything to deserve it, but the pain she was in certainly seemed hellish enough. Then the castle gates shut behind them and she was being dumped unceremoniously to the ground. She was so wracked with pain that she was having trouble remembering her name.

There was a heavy thump beside her, and Constance found the strength to turn her head and look to see what it was. She saw Suzanne lying next to her, out of breath and eyes closed. There was a pounding of hooves, and she saw the gate being opened again and the abductors riding out to rejoin the action. She dragged herself over to Suzanne. The girl was bleeding from the nostrils but seemed otherwise unharmed.

Constance hoisted herself to a sitting position. She had to use her arms, since her belly muscles were completely paralyzed. Sitting on the ground of the courtyard, she took Suzanne's head in her lap. She scooped up a handful of snow and began bathing her maid's face. After a few minutes, Suzanne's eyelids fluttered open and she stared up at her mistress uncomprehendingly. She tried to sit, only to have her eyes widen in pain.

"Here, Suzanne, I'll help you—don't try to do it yourself." With an arm beneath the maid's shoulders, Constance helped her to sit. "What happened, my lady? Where are we?"

"The robbers have us. They have an odd idea about how women ride—that's why your belly's sore." Suzanne's eyes widened in horror as she stared about her.

"They have us? What will they do to us, my lady?"

"Hold us for ransom, I suppose."

"They may hold you for ransom, my lady, but they know they won't get a sou for me. Oh, my God!" Suzanne gnawed on her knuckles and began to sob. She knew what was in store for her.

Constance looked about. There were only a few men in the castle, and those were atop the wall, watching the fighting and waiting to open the gate for the returning robbers. They were paying no attention to the two women.

"Listen," Constance said. "We don't have much time. You must watch me at all times and do exactly as I say. We're going to pass you off as a lady. It will buy us time and may save you from those animals."

"But I can't talk like a lady!" Suzanne protested.

"You won't have to. Just stay by me and say absolutely nothing."

"Yes, my lady," Suzanne answered. Then they heard returning hoofbeats.

"Let's try to stand up," Constance said. "It will do us no good to appear weaker than we are." Constance could not stand without assistance, but Suzanne stood without too much difficulty and helped her up. "At least your bandit had the wit to throw you in front of the pommel instead of on it," Constance commented.

Fulk rode in, red-faced and roaring. "Damned cowards!" he shouted. "Broke and ran when we had the treasure within our grasp!"

"We never had a chance at it, my lord," protested Pierre. "Not with this rabble on our side. Those men down there are the toughest I've ever tangled with. But they aren't going far for a while. Not with those wagons and this snow. We'll have them yet, my lord."

73

"Well," Fulk said, somewhat mollified, "perhaps you're right. Have to make an example of a few of the cowards, though. Pick out ten." Then Fulk's bloodshot gaze lit on the two women. He dismounted and addressed Constance. Absurdly, he prefaced his speech with a bow. "Delighted to have you as my guest, my lady. I see so few people of good birth these days. Your family must of course pay ranson if they wish to see you alive again, but that need be no cause for unpleasantness between us. Your maid can amuse the men while we have dinner. Nobody ever died of it, and you'll have her back almost as good as new in a day or two."

"This is not my maid," Constance said imperiously. "She is my cousin, Lady Ingrid von Kniprode. She speaks only German."

Fulk rubbed his chin as he eyed the girl. "German, eh? That's a long way to send for ransom. It could take years."

"We are on our way to Italy. Both of us are betrothed to Florentine nobles. They will pay our ransom. I need hardly remind you that no man who is concerned for his family name will pay anything for a woman who is not *virgo intacta*."

"Virgo in what?" Fulk asked.

"Maidenhead still where it belongs," Constance explained patiently. "No well-bred man has any use for a bride who can't stain the sheets on her first night."

"True," Fulk said. Then: "But he won't know until after he's already paid."

"Haven't you ever kidnapped a noblewoman before?" Constance demanded. "You know quite well they'll send a physician to examine us before handing over any money."

"Well, yes, I suppose they will. Anyway, you two

74

ladies go into the keep. I have to kill a few of my men now."

The two women turned and walked slowly to the brutish stone building, where a serving woman took them in hand. Behind them, the screaming started.

SIX

Falcon sat morosely, staring into the fire. When the bandits had gone and the train had been put back in order, they had continued for a mile or so past the castle until they found a small valley by the road which had enough level ground to pitch camp and a good supply of water and firewood.

Wulf watched his master nervously. Falcon was eating gruel like the rest, and he had a murderous gleam in his eye. Wulf had seen that gleam many times before, and it always boded ill for somebody. Finally, Falcon put down his bowl. The knights who shared the fire watched him expectantly.

"I want her back," Falcon said.

"Of course," Ruy Ortiz said. "A knight is obligated to rescue a lady of noble lineage."

"She wasn't part of the deal you made with the viscount," pointed out Rudolph of Austria, who didn't share Ruy's devotion to chivalry. "I say, let's cut our losses. We lost fifteen men today and we still have the wagons. Let's move on in the morning."

"I don't belong to your army," Bishop LaCru said. "I'm only here to oversee the papal tithe, which is still safe. But only an unworthy knight would leave anyone in the hands of those men back there."

Rupert Foul-Mouth came ambling into the circle of firelight. He squatted to warm his hands at the fire, and Wulf handed him a wineskin. The old engineer took a long drink and said quietly: "The lads're grumbling, my lord."

"Grumbling? What about?" Falcon's expression sharpened. Things had to be serious for Rupert to speak an entire sentence without a single obscenity.

"They think this is a bad-luck expedition. They think you've been taken advantage of by that viscount." He poked at the fire with a stick. "They think we've a right to take this treasure for our own." Rupert came from some island off the Frisian coast where an archaic dialect was spoken, but now he was choosing his words carefully to emphasize the gravity of the situation. The effect was more sobering than panic or vehemence would have been.

"They say that, do they?" Falcon said, his look getting deadlier by the minute.

"I'll deal with it, my lord," Ruy Ortiz said. He drew his long, heavy sword, Moorslayer. "I'll just go talk to the men, explain the error of their ways, maybe crop off a few heads. They'll see reason."

"Stay where you are, Ruy," Falcon said. "They're just talking for now. Time to chop heads when they come to us with arms in their hands. Just now, I have other things on my mind. Like it or not, I agreed to deliver that woman to her destination. I'm going to do it."

"Rupert, you've seen that castle. How long will it take to get us in there?"

Rupert scratched his gray beard. "Sittin' on that buggering rock, there's no tunneling. No decent wood hereabouts for siege engines or towers, so sapping the wall's the only chance. Maybe two weeks."

"Two weeks!" snorted Rudolph of Austria. "Even if the food held out that long we'd be trapped here by the snows. We'll be doing well to get down out of these mountains before the storms hit as it is."

"I know that," Falcon said, glowering. "Well, only one thing to do." Immediately, the faces of his men brightened. "Wulf, go round up Donal, Gerd, and Guido." He turned to one of the knights seated by the fire. "Sir Andrew, I want you to come along, too."

"Take me, my lord," Ruy pleaded. "You've never taken me on one of your castle sallies."

"That's because I need you in the camp, Ruy," Falcon soothed. "The men need a knight of your stature to look up to in my absence. After all, you and Rudolph are my lieutenants." This was only partly true. Falcon never took Ortiz on missions requiring stealth, even though, next to himself, the Spaniard was the best swordsman in the band. The fact was that Ruy could be a vainglorious fool and liked to think of himself as a hero from some poem. He was invaluable in a charge or an open assault, but hopeless in a sneak attack.

"Very well, my lord," Ruy said stoically.

Wulf returned with the designated men. Simon was already muffling the chain of his morningstar with rags. Guido had left his crossbow behind and had only his dagger, with which he was an acknowledged expert. Gerd had a number of curiously shaped small axes in his belt. He was a master of the vanishing art of the francisca, the ancient Frankish throwing ax.

"Um, beggin' my lord's pardon," Rupert began, with uncharacteristic hesitation, "but, well, I know ye'll have no trouble with the likes of them in that little dungheap

78

up there, bein's how they's naught but a collection of piles on a pig's rump, but—"

"But, what if I don't return?" Falcon finished for him. "Then you can split up the treasure and do as you like."

His men were silent as Falcon continued to stare into the fire. At last, he said: "Charging uphill. It's almost brilliant in a stupid sort of way."

Fulk finished hammering the red-hot spike and stepped back, away from the rising cloud of smoke, foul with the scent of burning flesh. The man didn't scream for very long. That was the last of them. The men had witnessed the punishment of their ten unfortunate brethren with equanimity if not outright enjoyment. That was what made these little salutary demonstrations so efficient. Not only were they good sport, but they taught the men a lesson while putting them in a good frame of mind.

Fulk tossed the mallet aside and went into the castle, brushing the snow from his shoulders. In the small, cramped hall, dinner was being laid. The day's exercise had sharpened Fulk's appetite and given him a powerful thirst. He found the two women already seated at the board. Both were working hard at looking fearless, but the German piece was having a harder time of it.

He seated himself at the bench and favored the ladies with a black-toothed smile as he grabbed a loaf and ripped it open. The women looked a little pale but otherwise little the worse for their ordeal. He signaled, and one of the serving wenches began pouring wine. Joints of pork, mutton, and veal were being brought in from the kitchen. Livestock in the neighboring villages was being slaughtered against winter's diminishing fodder, and from now until midwinter the eating would be good. Good for Fulk and his men, in any case. Whether the villagers made it or not was no concern of his. He noticed that the women were but picking at their food.

"Do not stint yourselves, ladies," he said. "Never let it be said that Fulk the Devil's hospitality is not generous." He carved a huge, dripping slab of pork with his dagger and dropped it onto the bread trencher which served Constance for a plate. She wondered whether he had wiped the dagger off since the last time he'd stabbed somebody with it. Fulk's men were filing in and taking their places at the table, turning the air even fouler than it had been.

"I thank you, Sir Fulk," she said, determined not to antagonize him. This man was an entirely different proposition from Draco Falcon. In spite of her unsettling experiences, her many aches and pains, and the unappetizing smells all around, she found her hunger stimulated by the savory steam rising from her trencher. She picked up the slab of meat with both hands and bit into it. Her confidence was beginning to return somewhat. Fulk would not kill them while there was profit to be had, and they might even escape rape. Things could be much worse.

Idly she watched the rats scurrying on the beams overhead. "Sir Fulk," she said, between bites, "we have not yet been informed of our accommodation. My ma— my cousin and I shall of course expect a private room, away from your men."

"You'll get what I give you, woman," Fulk said, then, more gently: "Please forgive me. It's been so long since I've enjoyed the company of noble ladies. Yes, there's a room on the top floor that should be perfect. I'll have it cleaned out and beds set up. Most of my guests stay chained in the kennel, but you will have only the best."

"You are too kind, Sir Fulk," Constance said, through

gritted teeth. Fulk waved a hand airily, dismissing his largesse.

That evening, ensconced in their tiny room, the two women went over their various injuries. The room was just beneath the wooden roof of the castle, and Fulk had given them a brazier of coals and hot stones to fight the chill. It made the interior smoky, but it was better than the cold. In any case, they had been raised in castles and were accustomed to breathing smoke in winter.

Suzanne unlaced Constance's tight-fitting dress down the back and peeled it down to her mistress's hips. With dismay, they examined the effects of her belly-down ride over the saddle. From her small but well-shaped breasts to the base of her pelvis, the white skin was an ugly brownish-black shot through with angry streaks of red.

"My God!" Suzanne exclaimed. "You're bruised so black I can't see your navel. It's a wonder you didn't burst something inside."

"If bruises are the worst I suffer," Constance said, "I'll burn a hundred candles to the Virgin next time I see a church." She massaged her belly gently with her fingertips, wincing as she did so. "How did you fare, Suzanne?"

The maid stripped down her own gown, revealing a considerably more voluptuous figure but only superficial bruising. "Not too bad, my lady," she said. She laced her mistress back into the gown. "Do you think they'll come for us, my lady?"

"I don't see how they can, Suzanne. The only way to buy us out would be by breaking open the treasure chests. As for storm or siege, I'm afraid it's only in poems and stories that knights go to war to rescue abducted ladies. Falcon must have lost many men today. Why should he risk more for my sake? I wouldn't ask him to, and I'm sure he's far too realistic to try."

"We're lost, then," Suzanne said, her shoulders sagging. "There will be no ransom, or your future husband will offer too little, and sooner or later these savages will grow impatient."

"Oh, we'll think of something before then," Constance insisted. "Maybe we can poison them all one night."

"That would be nice," Suzanne said, brightening. "Do you know anything about poison?"

"Not a thing," Constance admitted. "But I might be able to find out something. If ever there was a place for it, this is it." With nothing else to do, the two women lay down on their pallets and tried to sleep.

It had been difficult to make the proper reconnaissance of the castle. The crag upon which it sat was steep, the rock treacherous with snow. From time to time the snowfall would let up, and then the men had to crouch low and cease moving, lest they be seen from the battlements. Then, in the deepening gloom, they had made a dash for the wall. Against its base, they were screened from view.

They worked their way along the wall to the point at which it joined the keep. The old square stone tower was of rough stone, and had clearly fallen into ruin and been rebuilt by a succession of owners. The stone showed the marks of fire and catapult missiles. Falcon scanned the four-story tower.

"It's no Alamut," he muttered.

"What's that, my lord?" asked Sir Andrew.

"Just remembering old times. Guido, will you have any trouble with this?"

"I'll be up it like a squirrel," the Italian said. Among his other talents, Guido was something of an acrobat. With a coil of rope slung about shoulders and chest, Guido began climbing the wall. While hardly squirrel-like, his progress was fairly rapid. The age and crude workmanship of the structure, together with the damage it had suffered, provided him with holds for fingers and toes. So far, there was no sign of sentries checking the base of the walls or calling to one another. Obviously, they expected no attack from Falcon and his men. After all, the treasure had not been taken, and the ransoming of captives was a long-established business procedure.

Guido disappeared into the snow-flecked gloom. The others waited at the base of the tower. None of them wore armor, for fear of making noise. Falcon had his long, curved sword, Nemesis, slung across his back. Wulf had his falchion and buckler likewise slung. Donal carried his Irish ax and Gerd his franciscas. Sir Andrew had his odd poleax slung over his shoulders by a strap. Simon the Monk had his morningstar and a small, round buckler like Wulf's. All the men carried daggers for close work.

Falcon pondered as he waited. How many times had he done this? There was Alamut and Pierre Noir and that awful night at Valdemar's castle in Hattin. Those were only a few of them. Sometimes it seemed as if he'd entered more castles over the walls than through the gates. Then a rope came dropping down the wall to hang swinging gently in the breeze.

Falcon went up first. He was much heavier than Guido, and the climb was an ordeal, even with the assistance of the rope. There was also an element of uncertainty in this kind of thing. It was possible that Guido had been caught and killed, and the rope tossed down to see what would come up. In that case, the rope would be cut just as he reached the top of the wall and Fulk's men would laugh uproariously as he fell.

However, there was no problem. Guido was atop the battlement, sitting perched on a merlon. At his feet, a sentry lay in a widening pool of blood. Falcon glanced at the corpse as he pulled himself over the wall. "He made no sound?" he asked.

"He never even woke up," Guido stated. "God send us all such an easy death."

Falcon gave the rope a couple of tugs to signal the next man to begin climbing. Guido handed him a wineskin. "He'd been drinking this," the Genoese said. "Shame to waste it."

Falcon took a long drink. The flat roof of the keep was, of course, deserted except for themselves. The roof was of wood. In all probability, the stone tower was just a shell, and the entire interior was of wood. That was the common construction in all but the newest castles. One by one, the others made their way atop the keep.

"I smell food," Wulf said.

"Not surprising," Falcon commented. "They're probably accustomed to eating." He passed the wineskin to Wulf, and it made the rounds until it was empty. "Now," Falcon said, "if everybody is refreshed, let's be about our work."

"How do we find them?" Sir Andrew queried.

"We ask," Falcon replied.

They found a trap leading down into a guardroom where men snored on the floor. Against the walls leaned sheaves of spears and darts, quivers of arrows, piles of stones and other items for repelling invaders. There was a table to one side bearing a wooden platter which still held most of a joint of pork.

Falcon knelt by one of the men and clamped a hand over his mouth. The soldier awakened and tried to struggle to his feet, but Falcon held him without difficulty. He signaled to his men and the others died in their sleep. Wulf wiped his dagger on a dead man's shirt and went to the table. He brushed away a couple of inquisitive rats and picked up the pork bone and began tearing chunks off with his teeth.

"What are you doing?" Falcon hissed, still holding down the struggling man.

"I'm hungry," Wulf said. "Who knows when we'll see fresh meat again?"

Falcon turned back to the man he held. By now the others were pinning the man's arms and legs, and Falcon laid his dagger point to the man's eye. "Now, listen to me, my man," Falcon said. "Your only chance of living lies in your strict obedience. You will tell me where the two women you took today are being held. You will do this quietly, and with great accuracy. Do you understand?" The man nodded vigorously against Falcon's smothering palm. "Will you cooperate?" More nods. Falcon withdrew his palm from the man's mouth. The dagger stayed where it was.

The man pointed to a doorway that opened off the guardroom. "They're in there, unharmed. You're not going to kill me, are you?"

Falcon's dagger thrust like a striking serpent. He stood and sheathed the blade after wiping it. "Men will believe the strangest things when they're desperate," he said. He crossed to the door. It was of stout wood and was fastened with a heavy lock.

"I knew this was too easy," Falcon said. "I don't suppose the key is around here somewhere." A quick search of the room and the bodies established that the key was not present.

"Barricade the trap," Falcon ordered. The men rolled some heavy barrels onto the trapdoor that opened to the floor beneath. There was nothing to use as a ram, so they began to attack the door with axes from the stock of weapons in the guardroom. Although they chopped with frantic haste, the axes were for fighting, and lighter than woodsmen's felling axes. Slowly, the door began to give way, but they were making a great deal of noise.

Strange sounds dragged Fulk from his sleep. There was a pounding that wasn't part of the nightly routine. He sat up and rubbed his face. His pallet was laid on the straw that covered the floor, and rats scurried away as he sat up. "What's that racket?" he demanded. He threw an empty winecup at a sleeping man. "Go see what's causing that noise, you pig. Whoever it is, tell them to stop at once or I'll feed them their tongues."

The man got up to investigate. The interior of the castle was dimly lit by braziers and occasional candles and torches, although the light they shed was very nearly obscured by the smoke they produced.

Fulk's retainer returned. "It's coming from the guardroom on the top floor. The trap's been blocked and nobody answers my hail." This was odd. Fulk began kicking men into some semblance of wakefulness.

"Up and arm yourselves, scum! We may have visitors, and I'd not have them say I didn't give them a fine welcome." Quickly, he donned his own armor and headed for the ladder with an ax in his fist. He heaved himself up the ladder and placed a palm against the trap. It wouldn't budge. Grumbling, Fulk backed down. He separated some two dozen men from the mob waiting at the foot of the ladder.

"You men stay here. If they come down, kill them. The rest of you, come along with me. We'll wait for them outside. They'll have to come down sooner or later."

With a final smash, the door burst inward. They were greeted by two pale but composed faces. "Oh, it's Sir Draco," Constance said, fighting hard to hide her relief.

"Who'd you think it was?" Wulf demanded. "Fulk would have used a key."

"Wulf!" Suzanne shouted gleefully. She threw herself upon the Saxon with such force that the two of them staggered backward through the door.

"If you'll come with me, my lady," Falcon said. "Time is getting short."

"How are you getting us out of here?" she asked.

"Down the wall." He bustled her into the guardroom, where Constance had to raise her skirts a bit to keep them from dragging in the puddles of blood that dotted the floor. She stopped at the ladder and eyed it doubtfully. "I don't think I can climb it, Sir Draco," she said. "I had a rough ride today and I can barely move."

Falcon nodded to Donal, and the Irishman picked Constance up gently and slung her across his shoulder. His ax in one hand, the Irishman carried her up the ladder as lightly as if she had been a pillow. Falcon disentangled Wulf and Suzanne and booted the two of them toward the ladder.

Falcon went up last. On the roof, he found his men staring over the parapet. "Trouble, my lord," Simon reported.

"What is it?" Falcon leaned out over the wall. Indistinct in the falling snow, he could make out the forms of men below. There were a great many of them. "Damn," he muttered. "All right, everybody back down the ladder. We're going to have to go back through the castle."

"Why not just yield and arrange a ransom?" Constance said. "It was a brave attempt, but it isn't going to work, so why be foolish? You can't possibly fight your way through this place and hope to get away!"

"Madame," Falcon said, "there is no possibility that those men would let us live after what we did to them this morning."

In the guardroom, Falcon had the weights removed from the trapdoor. He leaned over to see below, then jerked back abruptly as a javelin came sailing through. Donal plucked the short spear from the air as it flew past and cast it back down. There was a scream from below, and the Irishman chuckled.

"I make it twenty, possibly twenty-five," Falcon said.

"Twenty-five!" Constance exclaimed. "You're only seven!"

"The room's no bigger than this one," Falcon said. "They won't be able to use their numbers."

"They're just scum, anyhow," Simon said, stripping the rags from the chain of his morningstar. "Shall I go first, my lord?"

"No. Wulf, you go first. You've done nothing but eat and make love since we got here. Go earn your keep."

Suzanne wept and wrung her hands as Wulf readied his falchion and buckler. Falcon lined the men up in the order he wanted them to descend, then he nodded to Wulf. The Saxon stepped to the trap and dropped through, ignoring the ladder.

The men below were not expecting the little band above to take the offensive. They were caught completely off guard when the man with the short sword dropped into the room and began cutting right and left. Someone thrust at him with a spear, but Wulf swept the thrust aside with his buckler and gutted the man. Another tried to grab him from behind, but the falchion spun dexterously in his hand and he stabbed backward, skewering the man neatly.

Then Sir Andrew was in the room. He thrust the point of his weapon into an armored throat and chopped into an arm with his ax blade. A man tried to rush him from the side, but Sir Andrew dropped to one knee and swept the charger's feet from under him with the shaft of Maid's Kiss.

In quick succession, Falcon, Donal, and Simon dropped in. Falcon had Nemesis out and was dealing wide-sweeping cuts with her curved blade. Each cut killed or maimed a man and sometimes two. The whirring, deadly spiked ball of Simon's morningstar was impossible to guard against and could get around any shield.

Through it all, Gerd and Guido kept up a continual rain of darts from above. These were two-foot spears with heavy iron points. Since they were too short to have a javelin's stability, their ends were feathered like arrows or had cloth streamers. Both were expert with all missile weapons.

Constance looked down with horrified fascination. She had seen knights fighting in tourneys and had watched occasional castle raids from the safety of a high tower, but she had never dreamed that this kind of murderous ferocity existed. Then all was quiet below. It was unbelievable. For all its exertion and concentrated savagery, the fight had lasted perhaps two minutes from the time Wulf dropped into the room.

"Come on down," Falcon called. "Guido, kick over the braziers first."

Suzanne helped Constance descend the ladder. They breathed through their mouths, for the smell of blood and entrails was insupportable. Falcon and his men looked like something from a nightmare. All were splattered from head to foot with blood. Incredibly, none of the blood seemed to be theirs. Some of Fulk's men were still alive and groaning or begging for mercy. Falcon's men were finishing them off with daggers.

"Do you have to do that?" Constance asked.

"Would you rather they burned?" Falcon said. Already the fire was crackling merrily in the guardroom overhead. Falcon and his men took rags and wiped their hands and the grips of their weapons, lest they become slippery with blood and sweat.

The party descended to the hall below. It was uninhabited save for a couple of serving wenches. They had overturned the braziers in the room above, and now they proceeded to do the same for the hall.

From the hall, a stairway slanted down the side of the castle to the courtyard. As in most such buildings, there were no openings at ground level. There were about ten men in the courtyard, craning their necks upward, staring at the battlement. This was what Falcon had hoped to find. The bulk of Fulk's men must be watching the wall where the rope still dangled.

Before the men in the courtyard quite realized what was happening, Falcon's band was among them and cutting them down. One bandit broke away and ran for the gate to give the alarm. Gerd stepped forward calmly and hurled a francisca. The little ax spun through the air and buried its edge in the back of the running man's head. Falcon and the others ran for the stables. Inside, they pulled horses out of stalls, snatched up bridles, and pulled them over the horses' heads. They had no time for saddles. Constance found herself boosted up onto the broad back of a horse, and then Falcon was mounted behind her, his arms around her waist, one hand gripping the reins and the other clasped against her belly. Falcon walked the horse from the stable, and then Constance's stomach clenched in agony as it broke into a trot, headed for the gate.

Fulk grinned up at the battlement from which the rope dangled. He hoped that they would give up and surrender. Then he could give them a slow death. His mind was occupied with devising new torments when he noticed the red glow coming from the top of the tower. His jaw dropped in dismay. "God's death!" he bellowed. "They're firing the keep! Everybody inside and get buckets!"

They ran for the gate. As they reached it, a party on horseback burst out, trampling several of Fulk's men. "Forget them!" Fulk shouted. "Save the keep!" Men dashed for the stable and came back with buckets. Others frantically hauled at the well rope. They were fighting to save their winter food supply and the roof that protected them. Without a castle, the band would be like a turtle out of its shell.

Men ran inside with buckets, and soon they formed a chain. Fulk glowered. There was no hope of saving the upper floors. With luck, some of the stores in the cellar might be saved. Above all, they had to keep the fire from building up enough heat to crack the walls. The wooden interior could be repaired.

One of the bandits came out of the keep to report to Fulk. "They killed all the men you left inside, my lord. They killed more out here and got clean away with the women and seven horses."

Fulk howled and hacked the man's head off in sheer frustration. That made him feel a little better and he turned to Pierre.

"I want them, Pierre. I want the women and I want the treasure and most of all I want that big bastard with the curved sword!"

SEVEN

To Constance's unutterable relief, they slowed down as soon as it was clear that there would be no pursuit. Not far from the castle, one of Falcon's soldiers held their horses and they dismounted and switched to the saddled steeds. Traveling at a leisurely walk, with Falcon's arm around her, Constance felt reasonably comfortable and almost safe.

The men were chattering volubly about their exploit, each claiming to have been the bravest and to have done the greatest execution. Constance saw that Suzanne was riding on the front of Wulf's saddle. The maid was holding the reins while both of Wulf's hands were thrust inside her bodice between the gaping laces.

Falcon followed her gaze. "Maybe his hands were cold," he said. Constance forbore to answer.

At the camp, they were greeted with cheering and jubilation. Falcon escorted Constance to her wagon and helped her make her painful way inside. She collapsed into the bed cushions, so exhausted she could hardly find breath to speak. As Falcon began to climb out of the wagon, though, she called to him.

"Sir Draco."

"Yes?" He turned to look at her. Her face was slack

with fatigue, but he seemed to detect more warmth in her expression than he had seen before.

"You once told me that you have never met a knight like the ones you hear about in the poems."

"So I did. They must be a rare breed."

"Rare indeed. But I think I've found one." Then her eyelids slowly closed and she began to breath deeply and steadily. Falcon smiled and left the wagon.

He called a meeting of his officers and addressed them. "We're not through with Fulk yet. We've left them without a roof in winter, and they'll be out for blood. We set out at first light tomorrow. While we're in these mountains, I'm doubling the rear guard. They'll want more than the treasure now. They'll be wanting our provisions, too. Now, go get what sleep you can."

Falcon was nearly staggering by the time he found his way to his tent. He found Wulf already inside and snoring loudly. He knew that it was less than two hours until dawn, and it seemed hardly worth the trouble of going to sleep. Still, two hours was better than nothing. Without being aware of the transition, he was dreaming. As always, he dreamed of the past.

Draco and Osman the Bedouin knelt before the dais upon which sat Suleiman the Wise. Their faces were outwardly calm and composed, but inwardly they cowered. The old man glared at them from under his tufted eyebrows. He wore plain robes, and his only outward distinction was the green turban he wore. The green turban was allowed only to descendants of the Prophet. Behind Suleiman knelt his sword bearer. Propped beside him, this honored functionary held the great sword Three Moons, the treasured heirloom of Suleiman's family. Seated around the periphery of the room were

Suleiman's officers and students, for he was at once magistrate, teacher, and military commander.

After a long, intense, and exceedingly uncomfortable silence, Suleiman spoke. "You two have disobeyed my command. You have taken it upon yourselves to absent yourselves without leave, to make a journey into hostile country, to undertake a mad scheme, and to commit a murder."

"We felt compelled to avenge your honor, oh Suleiman," Osman protested.

"Am I so feeble that I cannot protect my own honor, Osman?" The Bedouin had no reply. Suleiman turned his baleful gaze toward Draco. "And you, young Frank. Will you tell me what you have accomplished?"

"We killed the Old Man of the Mountain," Falcon said, with pride in his voice.

"Did you, now?" Suleiman said, raising his eyebrows. "Then how comes it that I received yet another threatening letter this morning from Alamut signed by the Old Man?"

"It's not the same one," Falcon said.

"And of what consequence is that?" Suleiman queried. "Today there is an Old Man at Alamut, just as there was before your mad expedition. The sect is not a beast that can be killed because you have cut off its head. What has your escapade accomplished?"

"We have dishonored them," Osman said fiercely. "We penetrated their vaunted stronghold. We struck down the Old Man in the midst of his followers. Such was their confusion that we were able to escape, though we went prepared to die. We have proved that they are but ordinary men, and their shame will last forever!" There were murmurs of approval and admiration from the men seated around the room.

"To whom have you proven this, Osman?" Suleiman

queried, gently. "This letter makes no mention of the incident. Did you think that the Hashishin would compose poems in praise of your deed? If you boast of your exploit, they shall say that you lie. Had you died after murdering the Old Man, none would have known of it." He glared at the two chastened men. Then he continued.

"Since it seems that this incident never occurred, then it would little behoove me to take notice of it. I cannot condone murder nor disobedience. However, since no transgression occurred, you escape punishment. This incident is now closed and I shall proceed with the business of the day, which involves some promotions. Osman."

"Master."

"Daoud ibn Gasim has become too aged to command my bodyguard any longer. You will take his position." Osman bowed deeply.

"Draco."

"Master."

"Omar's father has died and he must return home to manage his family's estate. You will take his position as my sword bearer."

Draco was stunned. Instead of being punished, he was receiving a high honor. He rose and strode to the dais, all eyes on him. Omar held forth the great sword, and Draco took it. It was the first time he had held Three Moons since the early days of his service with Suleiman, when he had been allowed to wipe blood from the blade. Just as then, he felt a strange tingling exhilaration from touching the fabulous weapon. It was as if man and sword had been created for one another. He knelt in the place vacated by Omar and held Three Moons propped before him. Once, Suleiman had hinted that one day Three Moons would be his. Now he knew that she had to be.

* * *

Morning came much too early. Neither Falcon nor Wulf had shown any inclination to wake up, so Rupert had their tent taken down and snow heaped over their faces. They sat up, sputtering and shaking their heads.

"Beggin' thy bleedin' pardon, my lord, but thy orders was most specific. We've got to move out now. Yon pig fuckers is going to be on us pretty soon."

Falcon glared at him. "Thank you, Rupert." The old man walked away, chuckling.

Wulf helped Falcon into his armor and went in search of hot water. Even in the most arduous of campaigns, Falcon tried to shave daily. Wulf brought him a bowlful of steaming water, and Falcon scraped painfully at his face with his dagger. It was made of Damascus steel, like his sword, and made a passable razor. After washing face and hands he was ready to face the day. He would have fought his way through another castle for a bath. His taste for frequent bathing was regarded by most of his men as exotic in the extreme, but he had been spoiled by the luxurious living of the East.

Falcon looked in on the women's wagon, but even the bustle of moving out had not awakened them. Ruy Ortiz took the advance guard, and then, lurching and groaning, the wagons departed. Today, Falcon took personal command of the reinforced rearguard. He ordered the Welshmen to ride out and look for pursuers. At midmorning they rode back with news that they were being followed.

"How many?" Falcon asked.

"About seven score," Gower answered. That was about what Falcon had estimated Fulk to have left. Yesterday's battles had reduced his force by a quarter of its strength. In contrast, Falcon had lost seven men killed and a dozen wounded the day before. Little danger of an open attack just now, then. But that would change. Fulk would dog them, and he would pick up new men as he traveled.

Just now, he had other worries on his mind. The men were looking sullen and resentful. It was the treasure. It preyed upon their minds and soured their thoughts. They were mostly common soldiers, poor men who had taken to arms as an escape from the grinding poverty of peasant life. The thought of this great heap of wealth was almost too much for them. It would be so easy to take it, and it would set every one of them up in wealth and luxury for life.

Which ones could he trust? Wulf, certainly; the two had been companions since boyhood. Donal was an old friend who had pulled an oar on the same galley with Wulf and Falcon. Ruy Ortiz was the consummate vassal, who would die under torture rather than betray his lord. The rest? He was pretty sure of Simon, Gerd, Guido, and the Welshmen. The other two knights, Rudolph of Austria and Andrew the Scot, would be loyal within reason. Rupert Foul-Mouth was a crusty old brigand, but he had thrown his lot in with Falcon and followed his fortune. In any case, it had been Rupert who had brought him word of the men's unrest.

Perhaps he was doing them a disservice. After all, they had proved their loyalty many times before. He remembered how they had come to rescue him at Goatsfoot, when through no fault of theirs he had gotten himself captured. Even so, they were only men, and this access to incalculable booty was something unprecedented.

In a way, he hoped that Fulk would keep up his pressure. That might keep the men's thoughts occupied and keep them from brooding upon their opportunity. If only they could get out of these dark, depressing mountains!

As the day wore on, the path began to descend. The

snow stopped falling and the sky cleared. The mood of the men brightened somewhat with the prospect of getting out into open, level ground once more. Mountains made for arduous traveling at the best of times, and they could be deadly traps in winter.

Of course, the flatland could bring its own risks. Fulk might have allies down there, or others might have learned of their mission. But then there was risk everywhere, and Falcon was accustomed to meeting it. It was his life.

He was shaken from his broodings when a small horse drew up even with his. To his amazement, it was Constance, riding her palfrey. She was swathed in a mantle of heavy wool and riding rather stiffly, but otherwise little the worse for her ordeal.

"I'm surprised to see you up and riding so soon, my lady," Falcon said. "I would have expected you to stay in your wagon for another day or two, at least."

"I come from good stock," she answered. "I'm told that when my father was away on a pilgrimage, a feuding neighbor came and stole a herd of our cattle. My mother was great with child at the time, but she just put on a fat man's mail and rode off after the thieves."

"Did she catch them?" Falcon asked.

"Caught and hanged them and brought the cattle back. I was born a week later. I don't remember her, as she died two years later. My father never came home from his pilgrimage. Since I had no brothers, I became the viscount's ward."

"And he's been getting the income from your lands all these years?"

"Of course. Why do you think I've remained unmarried for so long? He wasn't going to turn loose of a good thing until he had something richer to gain."

"This Italian you're to be married to—is he someone of importance?"

"That puzzles me," she admitted. "He's some Florentine noble. His family is an old one, but of no importance north of the Alps. I know of no trade agreements resting on this match. It seems unlike the viscount to let those lands pass into hands so far from his grasp."

"Peculiar indeed." Falcon had his own suspicions, but these he decided to keep to himself for the nonce.

"And you, Sir Draco?" she asked.

"Me?"

"Yes. Where does your story begin? I know that you went young to the Crusade, but surely you weren't born in Palestine?"

"No, I'm from Normandy. My family had an estate called Montfalcon, near Caen. We had a castle on a headland that overlooked the sea. I was raised there, and at the castle of our neighbor, Odo FitzRoy. I served my time as squire under Odo." A cloud seemed to cross his face at the name. "When I was about fourteen, my father joined the Crusade. He took me with him. Just before Hattin, he was betrayed and murdered by four men. One was the Gunther Valdemar I told you about. He was the one who captured Wulf and me and sold us onto the galley. Another was Odo FitzRoy."

"What became of Montfalcon?" Constance asked.

"I was believed to have been killed at Hattin. My mother had died while Father and I were Crusading. I have a younger brother, but Richard Lion-Heart seized the estate when he was raising funds for his Crusade. I don't know what became of my brother. He'd be about twenty-two now."

"What was he called?" she asked. This was fascinating. She had despaired of ever getting Falcon to talk like this.

99

"His name was Hasteinn."

"Hasteinn! What an odd name for a Frenchman."

"We're Normans, remember?" he said, smiling. "We're descended from Viking pirates. Some of the old names have been passed down in the families since Rollo took the duchy more than two hundred years ago."

"What about sisters?"

"One—she was called Alais. If she lives, she's around twenty. I've made inquiries, but nobody seems to know what became of them. The estate's in King John's hands, now."

"They say," Constance said, "that King Philip will have Normandy back in his hands within a year or two. If that happens, you could petition him to return the lands."

"I intend to. I did them a favor not long ago, and he's well disposed toward me."

"And in the meantime you'll live like this, a wandering warman whose home is wherever his army camps?"

"It suits me. I like wandering. It's the old Viking blood, I suppose. Besides, there are certain men I must track down and kill, and that quest is better served if I can travel freely." He said this smiling, but Constance knew that he meant every grim word.

"If I swear fealty to an overlord," Falcon continued, "I would never be able to take a step without his leave. I have no wish for such encumbrance."

"Your life would not suit me," she said. "Without ties of family and land, what are we? All of my ancestors have held land for some prince or other. What other way is there for wellborn people to live? I don't think I could endure such a rootless life."

"Pity," Falcon said enigmatically. Constance looked at him sharply. What had he meant by that?

Their conversation was interrupted by the arrival of

Wulf, who had been on a periodic visit to the advance guard. He pulled up beside Falcon and wheeled his horse so that it fell into step beside his lord's. "Open land ahead," he reported. "We're out of the worst of the mountains."

"Thank God!" Constance said. "Another day of bumping over these goat tracks and I should have gone mad."

"Wulf," Falcon said, "take some men and scout ahead for a good campsite. We'll need more than just flat ground if we're to sleep safe from here on. Look for something defensible. Even an old sheepfold will be better than nothing."

"Yes, my lord," Wulf said, and he rode off, shouting the names of the men he wanted to accompany him.

"Do you think he'll be able to find a place so high up?" Constance asked. "Someplace where we can set up decent tents instead of sleeping on the ground or in these cramped wagons? And I would give anything for a bath. I need to get into the habit, anyway. I hear that in Italy, they bathe once a month or even more often."

"If we find a good site, with plenty of wood, I'll get Rupert to rig up a sweat bath. It's not quite like soaking in hot water, but it gets the job done. The Turks prefer them. They use hot steam or heated rocks."

"That would be heavenly." The thought of such comforts, crude as they might be, seemed like the epitome of luxury after the stresses and privations of the journey.

They descended from the mountain crags into an area of low, rolling hills and valleys. The grass was brown, but it hadn't been close-cropped, and this caused Falcon some worry. It was good that they would have plenty of forage for the animals, but why hadn't the shepherds from the lowlands grazed their sheep here this summer? When good pastureland lay unused, it was a bad sign.

Wulf came galloping back from his scouting expedition. "We've found a good spot, my lord. It's an old ruined fort. There's still an earthwork where a palisade once stood, and a stone tower in pretty good condition. There's room inside the earthwork for the wagons and all the animals, and the tower can be made livable with a little work."

"Perfect," Falcon said. "Take Rupert and some of his workmen there and get it put in some kind of order. Is there water?"

"A good stream not two bowshots from the earthwork."

"Wonderful. We'll stay there for a few days. The horses need to rest and graze, and the men could use it, too. I'd like to reach the lowland more quickly, but if we have to fight Fulk again, we'd better not be exhausted. Oh, and Wulf . . ."

"Yes, my lord?"

"Tell Rupert to build a sweat bath."

Wulf blinked. "A what?"

"You heard me. A sweat bath. Now get moving." Wulf rode away, shaking his head.

By the time the main body reached the fort, Rupert and his men were well on their way to making the place livable. Work parties were sent under guard to bring timber from a nearby wood, and canvas was unloaded from the wagons to rig temporary roofing for the tower. It was a low, circular structure, only three stories high but unusually broad and roomy inside. Falcon guessed that it had been built in some past year as a border post to guard against incursion from the mountain pass they had just descended. Heavy siege equipment could not be transported over such a route, so thick walls were not needed.

By nightfall, they had settled in. Hearths had been

constructed and the men were warming themselves and cooking their supper. Sentries had been posted along the earthwork and atop the tower. The Welshmen had shot a couple of deer frightened from hiding by the wood-cutting party, and Falcon sat by the hearth within the tower, impatiently waiting for it to finish cooking. On stones lining the hearth, flat loaves of bread were baking. He held a winecup and listened to the fat sizzling as it fell onto the coals.

Wulf descended the ladder from an upper floor and reported. "You can see fires, but they're a long way off, back in the direction we came from. Fulk and his men must have set up camp as soon as they were out of the mountains."

"Nothing to worry about tonight, then," Falcon said. That was a relief. Rupert Foul-Mouth came in, brushing the dust off his hands.

"All ready, my lord," he reported. "Hot enough to roast thy bleedin' arse off in there."

"Good."

Sweating had never felt so good. Constance and Suzanne sat on a narrow wooden bench in the tiny booth that Rupert had jury-rigged as a sweatbath. Before them was an iron basket full of hot stones, still glowing from the hearthfire. They had peeled off their now-rank traveling gowns and were taking turns scraping each other down with a horse scraper borrowed from a groom.

"Easy on the belly, girl," Constance admonished.

"Sorry, my lady," Suzanne said, scraping down the once-white skin more gently. "The bruise is fading, though. Soon you'll be as good as new." She scanned her own body, which was now a glowing pink from the heat and the scraping. "I'm looking pretty good," she said complacently.

"Yes, you're lovely, Suzanne. Now, do my back." She closed her eyes and wriggled like a kitten under the rough scraping. "Suzanne," she said, "has Wulf said anything to you about Sir Draco? I mean, about what Sir Draco thinks of me?"

"Sir Draco? Why, no, my lady. In truth, on those times we've had together, he's found better employment for his mouth. He learned some marvelous things in the East. Do you know that he—"

"Yes, you've told me," Constance broke in. She wondered whether Falcon had also mastered these exotic refinements. "What I want to know is whether Falcon thinks I'm nothing but a haughty bitch."

"I'm sure I don't know, my lady." Suzanne was sincerely puzzled. Noble ladies were *supposed* to be haughty bitches. What had this to do with Lady Constance and Sir Draco, in any case? The lowborn frolicked when and where they could, and the highborn married for convenience and position. This love one was always hearing about was something invented recently by trouvères and had little to do with the realities of life.

"My lady, are you not to marry the Italian?"

"Of course I am. Why do you think we're on this journey anyway?"

"Then, what does Sir Draco's opinion matter?"

Constance fumed. She wasn't sure of the answer to that herself.

Wulf squatted by the stream, trying to keep from letting the snow wet his hose. Before him lay a heap of clothes and arms. At this spot, the stream had widened and deepened into a pool. In the center of the pool, Falcon was splashing about naked, rubbing himself down with a piece of coarse cloth. The temperature of the water was just above freezing. It was not the kind of thing Wulf would care to do, but he knew that his master was not quite sane.

"You're turning blue, my lord," Wulf pointed out.

"So what?" Falcon said. "My mother bathed in the river every day of her life, no matter what the weather. If there was ice, she just chopped a hole in it with my father's ax. Father didn't like that much, but he never argued with her when she was holding an ax."

Wulf snorted. "Normans! You're all crazy." He scanned the surroundings warily. If Fulk's men showed up, they were in desperate trouble. Leave it to Draco Falcon to take every precaution to ensure his men's safety, then take a mad notion to go bathing in icy water at sundown with no protection save Wulf. Where was Fulk, and what was he up to?

EIGHT

Fulk the Devil sat cleaning a pork bone with his black-
ened teeth. They were getting to the last of the provisions they had saved from the fire. Most of the flour and
cheese had been destroyed, and they had been using up
the meat from the smokehouse quickly. It was just as
well that the men were getting hungry. They would
fight all the harder when it came time to attack Falcon
and the treasure train.

He examined the men. Thank St. Dismas, most of them
had had the wit to put their gear on before running
from the castle that night. He'd put on his own armor
and helmet, so at least he wouldn't be helpless when it
came time to fight. There were still a few scraps of meat
on the bone when he threw it to the man who was
chained by the neck to a nearby tree. Jean the Chamberlain snatched it up and strove mightily to get his teeth
into something edible. Fulk roared with mirth when the
wretch began pounding the bone between two stones to
get at the marrow.

"You're a rare one, little man," Fulk said. "Not many
would try to hang on to a life as miserable as yours.

That's a difference between us, you see: We people of good breeding prefer death before dishonor."

He looked up to see a man on horseback approaching. Pierre walked the horse into the circle of firelight and dismounted. "I've spoken with your brother, my lord," Pierre reported.

"And what did dear Bors say?"

"He'll be joining you as soon as he can round up his men. They're out scouring the countryside just now."

"What kind of establishment does he have?" Fulk asked, pulling at a wineskin.

"He's got a strong castle right above the lowland road. The stables looked good, and he had at least a hundred men with him, not counting those that were away."

"Good old Bors. I haven't seen him in years, not since he murdered our youngest brother and stole Father's horse and arms and ran away to seek his own fortune. I knew he'd make out well in this world. You notice, we never got anything off travelers coming from this direction. Bors got it all first."

On the third day of their rest at the ruined fort, Falcon decided that it was time to move. "Winter isn't going to hold back for us," he told his assembled officers, "and Fulk will be gaining strength. We march tomorrow."

There was another reason for moving out, but Falcon didn't mention it out loud. The men were growing restive again. More and more of them were staring at the treasure wagons, muttering to one another, and following orders haltingly. Ruy and the other officers had had to strike men who spoke insolently to them, and that was bad for discipline. He was brooding on these matters when Constance came to him.

"Is it true that we're leaving tomorrow?" she asked.

"It is. The men and beasts have had enough rest now. It's past time that we were moving."

"I'll be sorry to go so soon," she said. "This isn't the finest palace I've ever been in, but it's been good to feel safe within walls again." Falcon walked beside her as she made her way toward the tent he'd had erected for her against the wall of the keep.

As they paused at the entrance, she said: "Will you come in and have some wine? It wards off the chill." Without demur, he followed her in. There was a brazier of coals providing light and heat. The brazier left a thick pall of smoke trapped in the upper part of the tent, so the two quickly sat upon the heap of skins and blankets and cloaks that served Constance and Suzanne as a bed. Constance poured the wine and handed Falcon a cup.

"Where is Suzanne?" Falcon asked.

"Wherever Wulf is. I don't expect to see her before morning. Your friend has robbed me of a maid."

"Then you'll need somebody to assist you," Falcon said.

"Assist me in what?" she asked.

"This," Falcon said. He took her by the shoulders and turned her so that she was facing away from him. With his big but nimble fingers, he began unlacing her gown down the back.

"Sir Draco!" she said, sounding not quite as indignant as she had hoped. "This is not proper!"

"You said I'd cost you a maid, didn't you? Is it proper for a noble lady to undress herself?" He examined the complicated pattern of laces which was gradually yielding to his efforts. "It's damn near impossible, for that matter."

She said nothing, but her breath deepened as she felt the tingle of his fingers going lower and lower down her spine. Falcon admired the graceful line of her back, curved as subtly as a hawk's wing, as he undid the laces. When the last one was freed, her back was bared to the base of her spine.

"There," he said, turning her back around.

"Thank you, Sir Draco," she said unsteadily. "Was there any other way you wished to assist me?"

"Yes." This time, when he took her shoulders, he pulled her tightly against him. She almost went limp when his mouth covered hers, but not for long. She was, as she had said, of good stock. Very quickly, she was responding as urgently as he. When he pulled her gown down to her waist, she struggled to get her arms free of the tight sleeves. Then she raised herself so that he could slip the garment past her hips and down her legs. She had never been naked with a man before, and she knew that she was supposed to be mortified with shame and guilt. Somehow, she was not. In fact, it felt more natural than anything she had ever done before.

Through half-lowered lids, she watched as Falcon stood and removed his own garments. His body was lean and hard, and so covered with the scars of weapon and lash that he looked like some striped jungle animal from a traveler's book. Then he was lying beside her and taking her in his arms.

He propped himself on an elbow a few minutes later and looked down the length of her. "Coming along nicely, I see," he said, gently stroking her belly. It was only faintly discolored now. She gasped as he leaned over and kissed her navel, then thrust the tip of his tongue into it. He felt her belly flutter against his tongue.

"Draco," she managed to gasp out. Then his tongue was sliding down below her navel and she thrust the back of her hand against her mouth to quiet the sobbing gasps she couldn't stop herself from making.

It seemed a lifetime later that he slid up along the length of her and took her in his arms again. Without awkwardness, he moved her legs apart and lay between them. She was so faint with pleasure that she didn't resist the first push of his entry, but then she stiffened at the sudden pain. She sucked in a deep breath, but his mouth came down over hers and stifled the scream in her throat. Then the pain was past and the full length of him was inside her, She wasn't sure how to move, but he set the pace and her own body seemed to do the right thing of its own volition,

He began slowly and gently, in long, exquisitely timed thrusts, but his rhythm built relentlessly, and by the time the ecstatic spasms convulsed her he was slamming into her with the power of the stallion she'd been thrown across during her abduction. Then she could feel every muscle in his body knotting as he pressed into her so powerfully that the top of her head was thrust against the tent wall and she knew through her daze that he was planting his seed within her.

The gray of dawn was beginning to show through the opening of the tent when Falcon slipped through. He almost collided with Suzanne as she returned. The maid sat by her mistress and began combing out Constance's long, tangled hair.

"By God, my lady, from the look of him I hope there's no fighting to be done today. He's hardly fit to couch a lance."

"Having couched it all night, you mean?" Both women giggled like young girls. Then Constance turned grave. "Could he have got me with child?"

Suzanne frowned and began counting painfully on her fingers. "No," she said at last, "you should be safe at this time, if what my mother told me is true."

"Thank God," Constance said, with relief. "How about you?"

Suzanne shrugged. "It's worth the risk," she said. "Anyway, it's easier with us than with you nobles with your blood and your pedigrees. Many a lowborn man wouldn't marry a woman who hasn't proved that she can bear children."

"You're lucky," Constance said sourly. Then she smiled and the two women compared notes until the men arrived to strike the tent.

Fulk watched the line of men and wagons as it moved slowly down the wide valley. The heavy vehicles left deep ruts in the relatively soft ground. At least there was no chance they would get away from him. He could have kept up with their snaillike progress on foot.

"Horsemen coming," said one of the men who rode with Fulk. He turned and stared hard in the direction the man indicated. Then he saw them: at least a hundred men, all mounted. A low line of hills hid them from the view of the train below. Fulk wheeled his mount and set out at a trot for the newcomers, his men trailing behind.

The leader of the approaching band caught sight of Fulk and held up his hand, halting his men. Fulk did the same when about fifty yards separated the two bands. Then Fulk and the other leader went forward alone. When their horses were head to head, they stopped. The other man wore fine armor. His helmet was conical, with a broad nasal that hid much of his face, except for a bristling moustache.

"Fulk?" the man said. In answer, Fulk unhelmed and threw back his leather coif. The other did the same, exposing a face so similar to Fulk's that there could be no doubt of his identity.

"Bors!" Fulk shouted, throwing his arms wide. The

two men embraced like wrestling bears, and both bands set up a cheer.

"Come, ride back with me to my castle, Fulk. We have much to talk about. It's good to see you again."

"Splendid. Shall I leave some men to keep track of our prey over there?"

"Don't bother," Bors said, turning his horse. "There's only one way they can get out of these hills, and it takes them right by my castle. I'm well situated, you see."

"Oh, wonderful!" Fulk said. The two men rode side by side before the now combined forces.

"How is Father?" Bors asked.

"Ah, that's a sad story," Fulk said, slowly shaking his head. "I fear I must tell you that he's dead."

"How did that happen?" Bors queried.

"Did you hear of the capture of Richard Lion-Heart a few years back?"

"Yes, I heard something of it. Taken in Austria, wasn't he?"

"Yes. Well, since Father was nominally his vassal, a man came to demand our contribution to his ransom. Father killed the fellow, of course, but not before he learned that the country's ransom train was assembling at Cahors. He tried to ambush it as it left the city. It was too well guarded, though. They broke him on the wheel in the town square."

"Ah, that is sad news indeed," Bors said mournfully. "I trust he died like a man."

"Never made a peep," Fulk said. "I watched the whole thing from hiding."

"And Mother?"

"Dead too. Remember what she liked to do to prisoners?"

"Aye, I recall." He laughed and slapped his thigh. "I remember the look on their faces when she started on them. I'll wager that sinners new-arrived in hell don't look that scared."

Fulk roared with laughter too. "Well, we took a man one day and Mother had just started on him when he up and died from fright. She started jumping up and down and turned purple in the face and then she keeled over, dead."

Bors chuckled. "That's how she'd go, all right." The two men passed the time trading family gossip until they reached the castle. The building proved to be a larger, stronger version of the border fort in which Falcon and his band had been staying. The earthwork was surmounted by a stone wall, and its central keep was square and taller than the other. The stables and other inner structures were in good repair, and there were a good many men waiting who cheered loudly when their master arrived. Fulk examined them and was pleased to see that they seemed every bit as savage-looking as his own men. He should have thought of teaming up with his brother years ago.

In the hall, they got out of their heavy armor and Bors called for food and drink to be brought. It was good and plentiful, but Bors bemoaned the passing of better times. "Time was," he said, "when I'd have had a sheep and a beef and a pig or two prepared just for us two, but things have gotten lean of late hereabouts."

"Why?" asked Fulk, setting his teeth to a mutton chop.

"These mountain valleys were full of shepherds and cattle drovers every summer when I first came here. Now they come no more."

"I'd noticed that the grass was uncropped," Fulk said. "What happened?"

"It's these louts I'm forced to work with," Bors complained. "I keep telling them: 'Don't take all, just the best. Leave them something to keep the flocks and herds going.' Do you think they listen to me? They're like children. They have no thought for the morrow. This was a paradise for men who have no use for petty service and work. Now I shall have to be moving on."

"I know what you speak of," Fulk commiserated. "My scum are just the same. I was already thinking of moving down out of the mountains even before this Falcon fellow burned my castle."

"What do you say, then?" Bors proposed. "As soon as we've taken this treasure train your man told me of, what say we head for the lowland? I've a mind to set myself up in some pleasant place by the sea where the wine is good and the merchants are rich. Shall we combine forces?"

"Done." Fulk and Bors shook hands on the bargain.

"Now," Bors said, "tell me of this Falcon. What kind of man are we facing, and what of his men?"

"He's a bold one," Fulk answered. "As tough and as brave as any I've crossed, I'll give him that. My lads hit him and failed to take the treasure. They did grab a pair of noble ladies though, and I was holding them for ransom like any other reasonable man. Do you think he sent people to negotiate payment?"

"Well, did he?" asked Bors impatiently.

"He did not. The bastard scaled my keep and came in through the roof, with no more than a half-dozen men. They snatched the women, killed two score of my men, set fire to the keep, stole seven horses, and got clean away!"

"God's death!" Bors swore. "This is no carpet-knight we're up against, is it?"

"It is not. Still, he's just one man, and his men are just men, and now we outnumber them by a goodly margin. When you see him, you'll know him by his sword."

"His sword?"

"Yes. I caught a glimpse of it in the fighting when we tried to take the wagons, then again for a moment when he rode from my castle. It's like no sword I've ever seen before. It's curved like a Saracen blade, but bigger and heavier than any such I've ever seen before. It's got a long hilt, and he uses it two-handed sometimes. From what I could see, the blade's got a mottled look. I think it's Damascus."

"Damascus," Bors said, fascinated. "A Damascus blade that big is a treasure all by itself. Forty of your men killed, you say. These are real fighting men we face. I have allies nearby. It might be well to enlist some of them for this task."

"That means spreading the loot thinner when we take it," Fulk said, doubtfully.

"Who says?" Bors countered. "Just because we make an agreement with someone doesn't mean we keep it. I'm stronger than any of them."

"That's good to hear," Fulk said. "I want to have the odds weighted as heavily in our favor as possible."

"Have you any idea of the nature of this treasure?" Bors asked.

"No. The man who told me of it was a mere chamberlain. He wasn't privy to his master's secrets. I think it must be gold, though. What else would make the wagons so heavy? The wheels are axle-deep in the ground now, and the ground's not all that soft!"

"So much gold," Bors said, greed casting a film over his eyes. "We could set ourselves up as great lords in the lowland, perhaps buy a county. Think of that, brother: a whole county to plunder!" They ate and drank, as dreams of plunder swam through their minds.

"How many did you see this time?" Falcon asked.

"A new band came in from the south," Gower ap Gwynneth said. "Thirteen men and one who looked like a knight."

The prospect was depressing. Every day brought news of new strength among their enemies. It seemed as if every rogue in the south of France was homing in on the treasure train, all of them like sharks with the smell of blood in their nostrils. It was beginning to look as if he was not destined to escort this treasure to its destination.

"Is this really worth it, my lord?" Wulf muttered. "Maybe the men are right. Maybe we should take this treasure for ourselves. It's not worth all our lives."

Falcon glared at him. "Not you, too. Is the thought of so much gold turning even you against me?"

"Never!" Wulf shouted. "Do you think there is enough gold in the world for that? But this thing is going to destroy us all. Admit you've been gulled and be done with it!"

Falcon smiled wickedly. "Do you think if we took this treasure for ourselves it would make the slightest difference to those men out there? Whoever claims the stuff, they plan to kill us all and take it. Have you and the other men thought of that?"

"Well, we could divide it and split up," Wulf said weakly.

"To be gobbled up that much more easily," Falcon pointed out. "We're outnumbered as it is. Our only hope is to stay together and use our discipline and training to make up for our lack of numbers."

"Well, yes, I suppose you're right," Wulf admitted. "At least while we're here and in danger. But when we get to the lowland and we've shaken these brigands, I think we should reconsider what we've undertaken."

"It's been a bad bargain, that I'll admit," Falcon said. Wulf was the only man he would allow to speak to him thus. In many ways, they were more like brothers than master and man. "But I agreed to this commission, and I'll see it through. I'll not have anyone else make a mockery out of my word."

A mischievous glint came into Wulf's eye. "Are you really abiding by the terms of your agreement?"

"What do you mean?"

"What about Lady Constance?"

"What of her?" Falcon said darkly.

"Didn't you agree to deliver the goods with the seals still unbroken?"

Falcon swung a backhanded blow that tumbled Wulf from his saddle to lie sprawling in the road, laughing and wiping the blood from his lip. Falcon rode on feeling better. That was more like it. That was the old Wulf he had always known.

As he rode, he fretted at the presence of the growing parties of robbers. It was not his nature to sit idle and wait to be attacked. He pondered what preemptive measures he might take. Attack and fire their castle? Not much chance of that now. Draw an attack and arrange an ambush? Possible, but ambush was always chancy when your enemy was better acquainted with the land than you. He much preferred these military ponderings to dealing with incipient mutiny within his army.

He reined his horse to a halt and watched his following go by. The men looked well enough, their minds, for the moment, on the surrounding enemy. The lumbering treasure wagons lurched and screeched by, then the provision wagons, some of them rolling along almost without protest. Falcon called Rupert Foul-Mouth to his side.

"Rupert, what's in those last three wagons?"

"Empty as a eunuch's codpiece, my lord. Them's for provisions, and we've used them up."

"Good. Even empty wagons have a use," Falcon said.

"My lord?" Rupert said, cocking a shaggy eyebrow.

"Just a plan I'm considering, Rupert."

"Yes, my lord."

"Go and find Donal and Bishop LaCru and bring them to me."

Rupert rode off in search of the two men. They arrived a few minutes later. LaCru looked at him sourly. In the small, close-knit army, it was already common knowledge that Falcon and Constance were engaged in a seriously sinful relationship. LaCru had been shocked, and was scarcely on speaking terms with Falcon any longer.

"You wished to speak with me, Sir Draco?" LaCru said stiffly.

"Yes. Bishop, this has been a rather dull journey for you. How would you like to take charge of a little mission? Something to stir the blood and bring the humors back into balance."

"A mission?" LaCru said, intrigued in spite of himself. "Do speak on, Sir Draco."

NINE

Bors watched the treasure train making its slow progress. He had been following the treasure for several days now, and he was getting impatient. He would have liked to attack as the train passed his castle, but he felt that he was not strong enough yet. He already had a two-to-one superiority in numbers, but an even greater disparity was more to his taste.

He was not alone as he watched. Henri the Depraved was there with his cutthroats, as was René the Fox. Ordinarily, they would have killed one another on sight, but the rich prospect before them made them allies. There were a half-dozen other bandit chieftains, each with a following of between ten and fifty men.

"Let's take them now," Henri was saying. He was a huge man, so powerful that he wore two coats of mail, one atop the other. Thonged to his saddle was an iron-headed club with a five-foot oaken handle. One of his men was charged with the task of keeping a spare horse handy at all times. Since the entire weight of man, weapons, and armor was somewhat in excess of four hundred pounds, he had to change horses several times each day.

"It's tempting," Bors said. "But there's still Enguerrand

the Rapacious to consider. He and his men haven't showed up yet. With his sixty or so, we'd have no trouble taking them."

"We're speading the booty thin enough as it is," René said.

Bors pointed toward the men marching below. "Look at those men. My brother's already told you how well they fight. By the time we've taken those wagons, there won't be all that many to share the loot." The others considered this glumly. Greed warred with caution in their iron-clad breasts.

"Look, René!" Below, one of the wagons was lurching, swaying precariously from side to side. Suddenly, it sagged on one side. Several seconds later, the watcher's heard a loud crack.

"They broke a wheel," Bors said. The others stared, eyes bright and feral. They saw men gathered around the disabled wagon, jabbering and gesticulating.

The bandit army, most of which had been seated on the ground, jumped to its feet. Bors scanned them and the other leaders. He knew what was going through their heads. It was the lure of a helpless prey. To such scavengers, the sight of a crippled foe was irresistible.

"Calm down, you fools," Bors said. "It's a wagon that's down, not the fighting men."

"It's one of the treasure wagons," Henri said. "Look at the tracks it was leaving."

"They're stuck," René said. "They must stay where they are or abandon the wagon."

"What difference does that—" Then Bors was talking to the backsides of horses as Henri and René began charging down the hill, howling like maniacs. Their men followed on horse and foot. Bors saw some of his own men doing likewise. Fulk came riding up to him.

"Did you signal an attack?" Fulk demanded.

"No. Those two fools lost their heads when the wagon broke down. "

"It *is* tempting," Fulk said. "I think now's as good a time as any to take them."

"We haven't much choice, now," Bors said. "But let's not be overhasty. If those two and their men are so anxious to fight, then by all means let them do so. We'll follow at a more leisurely pace."

Barking orders, they got their men together and tried strenuously to keep them from breaking into a run toward the fighting. Some of the minor bandit chieftains and their followings broke away and headed for the thick of it, as if somehow he who was there first would get a larger share of the loot. Bors and Fulk, under no such misapprehension, brought their men to the fighting in good order.

The defenders were making a rough time of it. The horsemen made short charges, wading in among the bandit footmen and hewing them down, then riding back to where their own foot encircled the wagons with a spear-bristling hedgehog behind tall shields. The bandits were unable to break in, and all the time, the archers and crossbowmen kept up their sleet of missiles.

"I'll get us in!" shouted Henri the Depraved. He dismounted and took up his club. Calling two of his men, he had them stand to either side of him, protecting his flanks with their shields. Treading heavily up to the shield-wall, he began bashing away. Even the stoutest shields could not resist his monster club for long. Slowly, men began backing away from his onslaught.

The archers began directing their fire at Henri, but their missiles would not penetrate his double-layered mail, and his helmet was an iron bucket that had only small holes for vision and breathing. The iron-headed bludgeon crashed against shields like a sledgehammer and splintered them. As men backed away from him, a weak spot was created in the enemy line.

"Do you think he's going to do it?" Fulk asked. He and his brother sat their horses on a high vantage point near the action. Their men had now joined the fighting, and they swarmed like ants around the embattled treasure train.

"If any man can, Henri will," Bors answered. "He has the brains of an ox, but he's the strongest man in Christendom, I'd wager."

"There's the man," Fulk said, pointing to a tall figure in armor that had just mounted atop one of the wagons. The man carried a long, curved sword over one shoulder and was directing the defense.

"That's Falcon, eh?" Bors said. "I've heard that name somewhere, not too long ago." He was distracted by the sound of a hunting horn. The man with the curved sword was signaling to his men. With fierce exultation, the brothers saw that the men were drawing away from the wagons. The oxen that had drawn the two sound wagons were dead by now.

Falcon's men were making an orderly retreat, keeping their shield-wall formation, with the mounted men and the other horses in the center. There was a moment of difficulty when they had to break the formation to get past the wagons, but the concentrated fire of the archers kept the bandits from exploiting this momentary weakness.

Then the wagons were abandoned. The fighting broke off and the bandits set up a cheer, shouting obscenities at their retreating enemy and capering about in triumph, ignoring the numerous bodies of their friends that littered the ground. Bors and Fulk forced a way through to the wagons. Fulk was about to climb from his horse into one of them when they heard Henri's shout.

"Not so fast!"

Bors turned to look at the iron-sheathed giant. "What's the matter, Henri?" he said.

"We saw how you held back!" René the Fox yelled. "You let us do most of the fighting, and now you are going to claim a greater share of the loot." René and Henri now stood side by side, and they were being joined by the lesser leaders and their men. The two brothers sat their horses with their men assembling behind them.

"There was no agreement to attack," Bors said. "You hotheaded fools took it into your thick skulls to come down here and fight. You can be grateful that we chose to follow and aid you."

"Aid? Grateful?" shouted Henri scornfully. "We did it all." He clapped his hand against his chest. "I was breaking their shield-wall all by myself. That was why they ran." He pointed to the force down the road, which was now mounting and riding away.

"Fool," Fulk said. "Do you think they would have run if they hadn't seen us coming to reinforce you?"

"Think what you like," Henri said. "These wagons are ours, now. René, go break open the chests and let's see what we've won."

René was about to climb into one of the wagons when Bors made a signal which he and Fulk had agreed upon some days before. Without warning, their men assaulted those of the other chieftains. The fighting was hard and merciless. Now, within smelling distance of their treasure, the bandits were almost mad with greed. There was little to choose between the bandits in the way of quality, but the men of Fulk and Bors were more numerous than the others, and they were prepared for this treachery.

René the Fox tried to scramble back upon his horse,

but Bors axed him down from behind as he was still half-way across his saddle. Men swarmed around Henri, but the giant swung his great club in devastating arcs, each blow splintering a man's bones. His shieldmen tried to protect his sides and back, but they were overwhelmed and killed in short order. Henri managed to get his back to a wagon so that he could keep his enemies in front.

A man in a barrel helm charged with an ax, but the club descended on the helm, buckling the plates and popping rivets, and blood gushed from the eyeholes and sprung seams. The surrounding bandits drew back in a half-circle. Treasure or no treasure, none of them wanted any further doings with this man.

Bors and Fulk looked at each other in disgust. All the other bandits and their leaders were dead, and only Henri was holding up proceedings. It was time to justify their leadership. The two brothers tightened their helmet cords and walked their horses to where Henri stood with his back to the wagon.

"Come and face me, cowards!" Henri said, his voice coming hollowly from inside his face-covering helm. Suddenly, Fulk spurred his mount into a lunge, his lance point held low. Henri jumped aside, avoiding the point and bringing his club down, killing Fulk's horse with a single blow to the head. Fulk got free of his stirrups and landed on his feet as the horse collapsed. Henri would have killed Fulk then, but Bors distracted him with an ax blow to the back of his helm. Henri whirled with amazing speed for such a huge man and swung the club at Bors's horse, but Bors reined the beast back. A safe distance away, Bors dismounted rather than risk his horse further.

As the brothers approached their foe on foot, the surrounding men watched the drama with great interest, as if it were being played out solely for their benefit. If one or both of the brothers won, then things would go on as before. If Henri killed them both, then he would become their leader. If all three died, then the men wouldn't grieve much and would choose one of their number as a successor.

Fulk and Bors closed cautiously from the sides. Crouched low behind his shield, Fulk darted in to aim a cut at Henri's leg below the edge of his hauberks. Even in mail leggings, a shrewd sword cut could easily shatter an ankle or shinbone. Henri jumped over the sword blow and whirled a devastating horizontal blow which Fulk barely managed to shift his shield to intercept. The shield was smashed back against his body, numbing his arm and spraying his face with splinters of wood.

The power of the blow was Henri's undoing. Its momentum swung him around so that for a moment his back was exposed to Bors. With both hands on the haft, Bors swung his ax with every ounce of his strength. The head bit into the mail over Henri's spine, snapping links and smashing vertebrae. The giant arched back, stiffened, and fell stiffly as a toppling tree. With his dagger, Fulk cut the helmet cords and pulled back Henri's mail coif, then stepped back as Bors brought his ax down on Henri's bull-like neck. It took three blows to sever the head, and the assembled men cheered as loudly as they would have had Henri been the winner.

"Now that that's finished," Fulk said, massaging his shield arm, "let's see what we've won." He and Bors climbed to the back of one of the wagons, their men pressing eagerly behind them. Fulk slashed through the canvas curtain with his dagger and tore it aside. His expression turned from one of exultation to one of dismay as he gazed inside. The wagon was filled to the top with stones, and the stones covered with a great heap of ox dung.

*   *   *

"I think the ox shit was a nice touch, don't you?" Wulf said.

"We can thank Rupert for that idea," Falcon said. Along with the rest of his men, they were watching from a slight rise of ground as the bandit armies rent one another like dog packs over a felled deer.

"It's worked better than we'd hoped," Ruy said. "There was always the chance they might find out about the wagons before they began to dispute possession."

"They'll know pretty soon," Falcon said. "We'd better be rejoining the rest." They wheeled and trotted off down the road. Two miles away, in a little stand of trees near the road, they found the treasure wagons. Bishop LaCru, who had brought them here under cover of darkness the night before, seemed almost faint with relief when they arrived.

"I don't think the Savior spent a worse night at Gethsemane than I've just had," LaCru said. "How did it go? Did you lose many?"

"Three killed and eight wounded," Falcon said. "When those scum back there finish fighting over the rocks and ox shit, they'll be weaker by at least half."

"Safe for a little while longer, then," LaCru said. "You've never known true care until you've spent a night and half a day transporting and guarding a fabulous treasure with a force of a dozen men and two women."

"Have the ladies fared well?" Falcon asked. By way of answer, he saw Constance coming toward him, holding her skirts clear of the ground, lest they trip her in her haste.

"How could you leave us here all day without protection?" Constance demanded. "Not only without protection, but sitting atop a treasure that draws murderers like sharks to a wounded whale!"

"We had an extremely delicate maneuver to accomplish," Falcon explained. "It was best done without the distraction of noncombatants."

"Distraction?" Constance was getting red in the face. "Is that what we're supposed to be, just distractions that might interfere when you warriors are practicing your trade? You—"

Amid much laughter, Falcon picked Constance up and slung her beneath one arm and carried her to the wagon she shared with Suzanne. Falcon tossed her inside. "You were safer here," he said. "But that could change at any moment. We aren't married, you know. Only wives get to speak to their men that way." He turned and went back to his horse, and soon the train was moving again.

Suzanne turned to her mistress. "You really shouldn't provoke him that way, my lady. I'd have thought that you would be overjoyed to see him back safe."

"Oh, I am," Constance answered. "But it would be wrong to let him go too long without an argument. He might start taking me for granted."

Fulk and his brother sat glumly at their fire. Their men sat all around, glowering and muttering. The brothers had lost much prestige as a result of the fiasco that day. Even though they had neither precipitated the attack nor allowed their men to suffer the worse of its effects, they were felt to be somehow at fault.

"They're as strong as ever," Fulk said, "and we have less than two hundred men left between us. Didn't I tell you this Falcon was a wily beast?"

"You did, and I can believe you now." Bors stared into the fire as if he were wishing for someone to cook in it. "And now I remember where I heard the name. A wandering poet came this way last year. One of his songs was about Draco Falcon. The man was involved in some siege a while back, and he fought a trial by combat with a great champion. I'd thought it to be just lies like most poet's drivel. I certainly never expected to see the man at my own gate."

"What next?" Fulk asked. "We don't dare attack him now. We're too weak and the men are in bad spirits."

"We keep dogging him," Bors said. "We'll pick up strength as we go along. And," he finished, smiling grimly into the fire, "there's still Enguerrand the Rapacious."

Falcon and his band could have wept with joy when they saw the town. It was not large, but it was surrounded by a stout wall and looked like a safe place to rest and find fresh provisions. They were coming down out of the pasturelands, and here the hillsides were terraced with vineyards. The town lay beside a small river and commanded a stone bridge.

"Does everybody understand the orders?" Falcon asked. "Nobody mentions so much as the word 'treasure' while we're here. We're a band of soldiers bound for Sicily to fight pirates. Anyone who lets slip our real mission I'll hang, be he knight or spearman. This is our best chance of decent fare since this journey began, but I don't want anyone getting so drunk that he loses control of his tongue."

"Sober soldiers will put them on their guard instantly," Bishop LaCru pointed out. "Who ever heard of such a thing?"

"It's a choice of evils," Falcon agreed. They marched down the road toward the town gate and were met by a local official, backed by a score of armed men who were clearly townsmen clapped into the ill-fitting gear of the town's arsenal. They all looked terrified at this prospect of some two hundred hard-bitten veteran soldiers all armed to the teeth.

"I am the king's bailiff for the town of St. Luc. Do you come in peace? If so, who are you and what is your destination?"

"We come in peace," Falcon said, taking off his helmet and lowering his coif. "I am Sir Draco Falcon, and these men are my vassals. We've just come through many days of bandit-ridden wilderness and would seek the shelter of your town walls. We're weary and in need of provisions, for which we'll pay well."

"Welcome, then," said the bailiff, smiling with relief. "But you did not tell us your destination."

"We're bound for Sicily," Falcon said. "The emperor's viceroy there needs men to help fight the Saracen pirates." A few years earlier, the German emperor had conquered the Kingdom of Sicily, which comprised southern Italy as well as the island of Sicily.

"I see," the bailiff said. "You may leave your beasts and wagons on the common just outside the city gates. The town has several inns, where your men may find lodging, though I fear there will be some crowding."

"They don't mind crowding," Falcon said, "but the wagons must come into the town with us."

"As you like," the bailiff said. "The courtyard of our largest inn will probably accommodate them."

They followed the bailiff into the town. Within the walls were huddled a great many low-walled houses, much like those of any other town, except that, as they were entering the south, most of the walls were whitewashed and tiled roofs outnumbered thatched ones. In his capacity as quartermaster, Rupert told off numbers of men to stay in the various inns while Falcon and his officers and the women proceeded to the largest, along with the wagons.

The inn was a long, barnlike structure surrounded by a low wall enclosing a courtyard. One side of the courtyard was formed by the front of the inn, which was two stories high, and two others by two lines of stables. Above the stables were rooms which opened onto a gallery. Falcon noted the stables with relief. He had been in many inns where the livestock was quartered in the common room with the guests.

Falcon saw to the positioning of the wagons and posted guards who were instructed to act as unobtrusively as possible. A heavy guard would have been a giveaway, but no guard at all would have been too great a temptation for thieves to look inside.

Within, the innkeeper greeted them effusively. It was late in the year, and travelers would be few until spring. This chance to fill the inn one last time seemed like a gift from heaven. "Yes, my lord," the innkeeper said, "I suppose you will be wanting the best rooms, will you not?"

"We will," Falcon said. "These ladies will require a private room, as will my man and I." He indicated Wulf with a wave of his hand.

"Well," said the innkeeper, with a Latin shrugging and spreading of hands, "that is not usual. We are accustomed to accommodating our guests five or six to the bed."

"You may change your custom for us," Falcon said. "We will pay the customary rental."

"In that case," the innkeeper said, "I shall be only too happy to accommodate you as you wish. I take it that you are hungry after your long journey?"

"Starving," Falcon said.

"We were not, of course, expecting to be entertaining so great a company this night," the innkeeper said, "so we have little food prepared. That shall be rectified presently. In the meantime, please make yourselves comfortable and we shall bring such poor fare as we have ready just now."

"Excellent," Falcon said. "I trust you have a bath-house."

"Oh, indeed. We have the largest tub in the county. It can accommodate six large men or nine small women."

"Fill it up, and make sure the water is hot."

"You shall boil like a lobster, sir. I take it that the ladies will want to use it first?"

"Yes, they will," Falcon answered.

"It's always so," the innkeeper said. He leaned forward conspiratorially and said: "It is believed by many that a woman can get with child by bathing in water that men have bathed in."

"Then we must be careful of our order of bathing," Falcon said. "I thank you for the warning."

He sat beside Constance on the long bench that ran the length of one wall of the common room. "Why are you smiling?" she asked.

"I've just been warned of the dangers of promiscuous bathing," he said. He told her of the innkeeper's comments on the alarming possibilities of used water.

"If Suzanne and I are with child," she said, "it won't be because of the bathwater."

The serving women brought baskets full of loaves of black bread baked from wheat and rye flour. There were also cheeses and tubs of butter and preserved foods such as sausages and smoked hams. As they addressed these, boys came running in from the butcher's establishment, bearing joints of fresh-slaughtered pork and veal. These were impaled on long spits and set turning in the huge stone fireplace at one end of the room.

There were pitchers of wine and ale and cider to make all go down easier. Falcon urged his men to stick to the ale, which was less likely to befuddle their wits. This was no hardship, as the ale was at its best at this time of year, before it had a chance to turn sour.

Falcon studied the few other travelers in the common room. Inns were usually good places for picking up information. There were some townsmen lounging about, but they held little interest for him. He was looking for people who had been traveling recently. There was nobody present who looked like a merchant. That was to be expected. Merchants would have returned home by this time of year. Then he saw a plainly dressed man who wore a leather cap covered with embossed seals of thin lead. These were the signs of various holy sites sought out by pilgrims.

"Wulf," Falcon said, "invite that pilgrim to our table."

There was no way of guessing the man's station by his dress. Pilgrim's invariably dressed plainly, and were supposed to make no show of worldly vanity. Falcon had met princes dressed in homespun and journeying with peasants to the holy sites. This one came to their table and bowed ceremoniously. Falcon motioned for the man to take the place vacated by Wulf.

"I thank you for your kind invitation, sir," said the pilgrim. His voice was heavily accented, but his manners were refined. "I am Francesco Gonzaga, from the town of that name in Lombardy. I am at present on pilgrimage to the shrine of St. James of Compostela."

Falcon introduced himself, Lady Constance, and his principal officers. He made only casual conversation until the pilgrim had clearly eaten enough to take the sharpest edge off his hunger. Anything more hurried would have been unforgivably bad manners.

As they traded small talk, the main courses arrived. Falcon selected a leg of veal and placed it on his trencher. Constance, still feeling the privations of the journey, and all too aware of more to come, picked up a roast goose in both hands and bit into it, being careful to lean well over her trencher so that it would soak up the juices.

Gonzaga drew the dagger which was sheathed in a pouch laced to his purse and used its pommel to crush in the top crust of a pork pie. With its point, he daintily speared out chunks of pork and ate them, pausing from time to time to dip a piece of bread into the savory juices, which smelled of pepper and thyme.

At last, all were replete and it was permissible to open serious conversation. "Tell me, good pilgrim," Falcon began, "in your travels hither from Italy, did you happen to cross a rather substantial fief called Forêt-St.-Denis?"

"Indeed I did," answered Gonzaga. "It is held by the Viscount of Limoges, although he has not visited the place in many years, I was told. I received hospitality at three small castles on the fief as I walked hither. It is kept for the viscount by a knight called Sir Maurice de Burgh. He is a most courteous gentleman."

"How far is it from here to the border of Forêt-St.-Denis?" Falcon asked.

"It lies about ten days south of here, at a walking pace," Gonzaga said.

"I fear that a walking pace is as much as we can manage," Falcon commented ruefully. "Is the border marked in any way?" Often there was no way to know when one crossed from one fief, or even one kingdom, into another, until one was challenged by soldiers.

"There is no marker, but you will not mistake the border. You will come to a bridge of stone crossing a deep chasm called the Gorge of Lost Souls."

Constance looked at him sharply. "That sounds like an ominous place."

"Merely a colorful local name, my lady," the pilgrim said. "It has something to do with a tribe of Christians

133

who were martyred there by King Clovis of the Franks in the years before his conversion. I assure you, it's quite safe. The bridge is an exceptionally fine one, built by the Romans and still as good as new."

"I hope the martyrs have long since departed and taken up residence elsewhere," Constance said. She rose from the table. "If you will excuse me, my maid and I shall seek that bathhouse."

That evening, Falcon, Wulf, Sir Ruy Ortiz, Sir Andrew, and Sir Rudolph of Austria sat stewing in the slightly used water. They spoke of their plans as they passed around a skin of white wine.

"It will be mostly open country from here on," Falcon was saying. "We won't be as vulnerable as we were in the mountains."

"Just as slow, though," Rudolph pointed out. "What's to stop Fulk from going ahead of us and joining with others, to wait for us to come to him? He could be ahead of us right now."

"That's possible, of course," Falcon said. He took a long pull at the wineskin and passed it to Wulf. "We'll just have to fight harder than they do."

Constance closed her eyes and ground her hips down as forcefully as she could. Her knees were planted on the bed astraddle Falcon's waist, and she leaned forward, her hands clutching his hard-muscled shoulders as his own hands gripped her waist. Her mouth was wide open, gasping as if she were drowning. She met his every upward lunge with the whole weight of her body, and still she couldn't get enough. It seemed as if the ultimate, ecstatic moment would elude her this time. Then Falcon pulled her down hard against him and moved her slowly and powerfully, and the shuddering waves broke through her body and left her collapsed in a heap on his chest, utterly limp and drained.

At last, when she had breath to speak once more, she said: "Is it sinful to take so much pleasure in loving?"

"The priests will tell you it is," Falcon answered, running a callused hand up and down her back. "Whether you believe them is your affair."

"I've always been told to believe them," Constance said, her fingertip tracing circles on his shoulder. "But I think they must be wrong about this. How can anything that feels so good, so *right*, be sinful?"

"You tell me. I've been told by priests that I'm more than half pagan anyway."

"Well," Constance said teasingly, "you *were* taught by unbelievers, weren't you?"

"By Saracens and Jews." He laughed briefly. "Believe me, Constance, they have as many peculiar beliefs as Christians."

She turned serious. "Draco, what will we do when we reach Forêt-St.-Denis? What becomes of us?"

"That is up to you. So far, I've had little thought to spare for anything but getting us there alive. Against my will, I agreed to deliver you there along with the treasure. If it is at all possible, I shall do so. After that, you may proceed to your betrothed in Italy if you wish. I have no say in the matter."

"And if I would rather stay with you?"

"That also is your choice. But remember: You would lead the same life I lead, that of a wandering soldier. It may be many years before I have a fief of my own. It means living in a tent, bearing children in a wagon, and being separated from me for long periods. I've seen women living that life in Palestine. The ones who survive age quickly."

She pillowed her head on his chest and settled herself

more comfortably. She still felt mild tingles. "Well, I still have ten days to think about it." Then she saw that he was asleep. His hands twitched and clenched, and she knew that he was having another of his troubled dreams.

TEN

Draco de Montfalcon rode his gelding through the shimmering desert heat of summer, baking inside the fine armor his master had had made for him by the best mailsmith in Damascus. Beside him rode Wulf, and before them both was Suleiman the Wise. For three years now, he had ridden or walked at Suleiman's back, keeping the great sword Three Moons ready should his master need her.

Behind them rode the black-bearded bodyguards, led by Osman the Bedouin. All rode fine horses and wore white robes over their light armor. They were on their way to Mecca, in southern Arabia near the shore of the Red Sea. Suleiman wished to make a last pilgrimage before he died.

The Damascus-Medina road was one of the great trade routes of the Islamic world, and most of the year it was crowded with merchants and pilgrims. Even so, it was dangerous to travel. There was always the chance of ambush by Crusaders, or by diehard adherents of the Ismaili Shiite caliphs of Egypt, the Fatimids, who still hoped to regain their caliphate. Then there were always plenty of outlaws, innocent of any religious or political motivation.

At this time of year, when the weather was good and the winds favorable, most pilgrims bound in their direction would board ship at Aqaba for the easy sail to Jedda, the port near Mecca. Suleiman, however, was on a tour of inspection as well as a *hajj*, and would be dropping in on the magistrates of the cities along the route. These cities had grown wealthy on the trade of the pilgrims, and woe unto any official found guilty of corruption by Suleiman. The Abbasid caliph had given Suleiman instructions to make inquiries during his *hajj*.

Already, they had passed through Wadi el Retem, Qal'at el Mudauwara, and Dhat al Hajj. Their next stop would be Mahtab, and after that, Tebuk. Along the way, the procession attracted many stares. Those who trod the route were accustomed to strange and exotic sights, but to see a descendant of the Prophet followed by a pair of huge Franks was unprecedented. Whenever they were seen, men made signs against the evil eye toward Falcon and Wulf. To the dark men, their pale skin, their blue eyes, and Wulf's yellow hair gave them the aspect of ghosts. When Draco lowered his mail coif to reveal his bizarre white streak and scar, the effect was multiplied. Suleiman's friends had advised him against having such obvious savages in his following, but he had said that even the most barbaric of men could be taught.

Draco rode with long stirrups, so that his legs hung nearly straight on each side of his horse. With his long legs, he had never accustomed himself to the Saracen style of riding with the knees sharply bent. Riding as he was, should an enemy appear, he need only lower his lance, snapping the butt under his arm and tight against his side, and charge. The long stirrups and high-cantled saddle welded man, horse, and lance into a remorseless engine of destruction. He was riding just now with his coif thrown back, his helmet hanging from his saddle.

Three Moons was sheathed across his back as his eyes shifted restlessly, seeking to penetrate the shimmering heat haze that made vision so difficult at any distance.

Osman the Bedouin rode past Draco to confer with Suleiman. "Master, I counsel that we wait out the heat of the day at the oasis." He referred to a small oasis halfway between Dhat al Hajj and Mahtab. It was too small to support a village, but it was used by all travelers on the road. They were due to reach it just after midday. "The heat devils will not let us see more than a hundred paces. Let's wait until it's cooler to set out again. We will still reach Mahtab before nightfall."

So, Draco thought, even a desert hawk like Osman was distressed by the visibility. He was always chaffing Draco and Wulf, saying that their blue eyes were not good for seeing in the blinding desert glare, and that only brown-eyed men belonged in the great sand wastes. It seemed that his brown eyes served him no better under these conditions.

"Besides," the Bedouin went on, "the horses are not used to this heat and should rest. Camels would have been a better choice for this journey."

"I think, Osman," said Suleiman, "that had the *hajj* not been arduous, the Prophet would not have demanded it of us. Of what use is devotion demonstrated only by performing simple and easy acts? Nevertheless, I agree that it would be a sound idea to wait out the heat at the oasis."

Draco was relieved to hear the exchange. Tough as he was, riding in armor beneath the blistering sun was an almost unbearable ordeal. Wulf rode beside him in a short mailshirt which was fractionally cooler than the long hauberk Draco wore. The Saxon too had doffed his helmet, and rode with the cowl of his white *jubbah* pulled over his head against the sun.

"I'll be glad to stop for a while," Wulf said. "I'm getting blisters on my butt. Maybe I'll cool it off in the spring at the oasis." He spoke in the rough camp French of the Crusaders, the tongue he and Draco always used between themselves.

"Dunk your tail in that stream," Draco said, "and the Saracen's will skin it and make a drum from the skin. They don't care to have their water defiled out here where it's so scarce."

Wulf shrugged irritably. "What's so wonderful about clean water, anyway? We never bothered about it back home." He stared at the road ahead. "Where are all the travelers?"

"What?" Draco said.

"The travelers. You know—the merchants and the returning pilgrims. Yesterday the road was choked with them. Early this morning, there were plenty. I haven't seen anyone coming from ahead in quite a while. I don't know when they stopped."

Mentally, Draco kicked himself for not noticing it himself. "Probably they're doing just what we plan to: They're waiting out the worst of the heat at the oasis. We'll find a crowd there, most likely." Still, it was a matter worthy of note, and he rode up to Suleiman, who was still speaking with Osman.

"Master," Draco said, "there have been no travelers passing us from ahead in some time. Most likely, they are all waiting at the oasis, but I thought I should mention it." Instantly, Osman's eagle gaze swept the rocky terrain ahead. He wheeled his lithe mount and rode back to the bodyguard and began shouting orders at them.

"I had noticed this since midmorning," Suleiman said. "I was wondering when it would come to your attention." For a moment, Draco said nothing. He wasn't going to admit that he hadn't noticed at all.

"Do you wish to take Three Moons?" Draco asked.

"No, I have my bow, should there be danger. I have never mastered the knack of using Three Moons from horseback." Suleiman took his bow from its case and handed it to Draco. Stringing the powerful, recurved bow in the saddle was a difficult task for the old man, but the big young Frank hooked one end under his thigh and bent the bow in his powerful hands until he could push the string into the upper nock. He handed it back and Suleiman replaced it in its case, now ready for instant use.

Osman had ordered picked men of the bodyguard to ride to the flanks with bows strung while the lancers closed up and rode just behind Suleiman. The old man noted these precautions with favor. "More than likely it is nothing," he said, "but it is never amiss to be careful."

Draco pulled up his cloth-lined mail coif, wincing when the edges of his sun-heated mail touched his skin. He pulled its veil across his face and tied it to the temple with a leather lace. With the veil in place, only his eyes were visible. He clapped on his helmet and tied its chin cord. Then he thrust his mailed left arm through the straps of his long, kite-shaped shield and adjusted their fit. Last of all, he took his lance from its saddle boot and was ready for whatever might befall him.

At first, the oasis was a shimmery smudge looming in the distance. The tops of date palms danced and writhed like spiders, and the shapes of shrubs, beasts, and men were so indistinct that it was impossible to make any kind of count. Even through the muffling of his coif, Draco could tell that there was too little sound coming from the oasis. He heard only the noises of camels and horses. There should have been a bedlam of shouting and chatter as various parties arrived and left, greeting one another or making their farewells and always cursing or praising their beasts. If the sound of voices was insufficient, another sound was in all too great supply: the faint clink of metal against metal.

"Armed men ahead," Draco called quietly. "Many of them." They slowed their already slow pace to the barest walk. Gradually, the air ahead cleared until they could see clearly. There were a great many people assembled at the oasis. They wore all sorts of clothing, from that of camel drivers to that of doctors. Nowhere could Draco see a sign of a weapon. The people stood huddled together, staring at the approaching men with wide eyes and making no sound. Suleiman held up his hand and his men halted.

"They will attack now," Suleiman said, as if he were announcing a change in the weather. "Do not kill them all, my children. We must know who sent them."

A high-pitched ululation rang out from behind the crowd of men on foot. With amazing suddenness, a line of helmeted men appeared from behind the pilgrims. They had been lying down with the pilgrims hiding them from view, each man holding his horse's head against the ground, one leg across his saddle. At the signal, all the horses had lurched to their feet at once. At another shrill cry, they charged forward, trampling many of the unfortunate pilgrims who could not scramble swiftly enough from their path.

Osman yelled orders and drew his sword. He rode to Suleiman's side. The Bedouin waited like a statue with scimitar and buckler, ready to lay down his life for his master. Suleiman calmly raised his bow, drew, and loosed, just as if he were practicing on the target range at home. A man in a black headcloth and veil tumbled from his horse.

Draco wanted to stay by Suleiman, but he knew that his Frankish style of fighting was best exploited while in violent motion. He turned to Wulf. "Stay by the master," he barked. The Saxon nodded and slipped from the saddle. With his short sword drawn and his buckler on his left forearm, he stood by Suleiman's right stirrup as Osman stood on his left.

Draco dug in his spurs and charged straight for the center of the enemy line. There were at least fifty of them, all in the black veils. Osman's archers were beginning to bring them down, but they seemed even more disconcerted by the outlandish sight of a huge Frankish knight charging down on them with lance couched. One of them, braver than the rest, swerved and charged Draco.

The black-veiled man carried a small round shield of tough hide and bore a light lance. "Die, Nazarene!" he screeched.

At the last second, Draco stood fully in his stirrups, jerked the edge of his shield to eye level, and clamped his lance tightly against his side. Even before he felt the other man's point skitter harmlessly off his tough, heavy shield, he felt his own smash through the opposing shield as if it were parchment. The terrible steel point, with the full weight of horse, man, and armor behind it, crunched through the light mail, through ribs and backbone, and then three feet of the lance stood out behind the desert raider. He shot backward off the saddle and for a moment hung there like a speared fish, then lance and man crashed to the ground. Draco heard Suleiman's guards cheering his feat, then he was through the enemy line.

He had had to release the lance, as there was no chance of freeing it. By the time he had slowed his horse enough to turn and ride back, he was at the edge of the oasis, and men were staring at him wide-eyed, as if he were some apparition from another world. In a way, he was.

Turning, he saw that the fighting was furious around Suleiman. As he rode back, he reached for the scimitar he wore belted to his left side. Somehow, it was not there. He took a look down, and saw that his shield had snapped back against the scabbard when it was struck, breaking one of the slings that held the scimitar to his belt. Now the weapon dangled out of his reach. There was no sense in trying to fight with his dagger. He had only one weapon left. Hoping that Suleiman would forgive him, Draco reached behind his shoulder and whipped Three Moons from her sheath. Only a man with his remarkable length of arm could have drawn it from such a position.

With the great sword in his hand, he felt like a giant. He had never held her in battle before, though Suleiman had permitted him to swing her in practice a few times, and had even had a practice sword made that resembled her so that Draco could get used to her feel. But the real sword was something else entirely. She seemed to come alive in his hand, thirsting for blood. For the first time since losing his father, Draco found himself roaring out the de Montfalcon battle cry: "Strike, falcons! Strike, falcons!" Yelling like a maniac, he plowed into the knot of struggling men surrounding Suleiman.

The first to die was a man who could not wheel his horse quickly enough to face Draco. The young Frank simply rode him down, the man's small gelding being bowled over by Draco's much bigger mount. Draco's mount's forehooves took care of finishing the desert man off. In the confusion, Draco saw that Suleiman was still mounted, encircled by his bodyguards, and that Wulf still stood by him while Osman directed the defense. They were hard pressed and the situation was desperate.

Another raider turned to face Draco and sliced at him with his scimitar. Draco let the light blade glance from his helmet and replied with a horizontal cut that sheared through the thin mail as if cutting cloth. The man doubled over, spraying blood. Another attacked from his shield side. It was difficult to swing the big sword across his body, as his shield got in the way. Draco tried to wheel his horse to the left and get the man directly in front or even better to the right, but the man was a wily, experienced fighter and stuck to the position that gave him the best advantage.

Infuriated, Draco slipped his forearm from the shield straps and cast the heavy defense directly at his opponent. The man was taken by surprise and had to raise both arms to ward off the unorthodox missile. As he did, Draco took Three Moons in both hands and swung her across and down. The heavy blade removed an arm and bit into the chest, smashing the man backward onto his horse's rump and thence to the ground.

Two more men rode at Draco, one from each side. It was impossible to avoid the cuts of both swords, so he ignored them, concentrating on killing his enemies and trusting to his superior armor to protect his body. He disposed of the men with two terrific chops, hurling them from their saddles to be trampled beneath the flailing hooves of the frantic horses. As soon as they were down, he rode in search of more. Rarely did he need more than a single blow to kill or maim an enemy. The great sword seemed to lend strength to his arm and precision to his eye. Suleiman had told him many times that the curved, razor-sharp blade was to be used with delicacy and finesse, but generations of ferocious ancestors urged him on to devastating blows.

The heat and the clouds of dust, the cries of dying men, the ringing of steel, and the shrill screams of the horses made a chaos in which it was difficult to discern who was winning. After making sure that no enemy was riding upon him from behind, Draco rode a little way off from the fighting to get a good overall view of what was happening and where his services were most needed.

From a little rise a few hundred paces from the action, he could see that the attackers were now down to about twenty men, and that they were outnumbered by Suleiman's guard. He saw Suleiman, now afoot, with Wulf at his back. Apparently, Suleiman's horse had been killed or had thrown him. Osman and most of the others were still mounted and were fighting fanatically to annihilate the enemy. Then Draco saw something unbelievable.

Calmly, as if he were taking a stroll in his own garden, Suleiman simply walked away from the circle of his guard. It was so unexpected that at first nobody noticed it. He walked away from the action about a hundred paces toward where Draco sat, watching without belief. Then the old man stooped down to help one of his fallen guards to stanch the blood of a wound. Draco could see the wounded man gesturing for his master to go back to the protection of his guard.

Wulf was the first to notice Suleiman's defection. He looked all about him, even searched the ground to see if his master had fallen. Even at such a distance, Draco could see the Saxon's mouth fall open when he spotted Suleiman a hundred paces away, tending to a wounded man. Wulf began tugging at shoulders frantically, pointing to where Suleiman crouched beside the guard. There were howls of dismay, and Osman tried to organize the men to go to their master's aid while keeping the remaining attackers engaged. Wulf waited no longer, but set out at a run.

The Saxon was not the only one to have noticed. A black-veiled man on a horse finer than the rest spotted the man in the green turban and wheeled his horse, setting off at a gallop. Draco dug in his spurs at the same instant. His mount, tired and winded, showed its spirit by bounding off like the wind, inspired by his urgency.

The raider was plainly the leader. His arms and helmet were as superior as his mount. On his left arm was a gold-chased round shield, and above his head he held a lean scimitar. He sped past Wulf as if the Saxon were standing still. Desperately, Wulf threw his falchion at the raider's back, but the man was riding away from him too fast for it to strike. Draco spurred his mount to even greater speed. He took his reins in his teeth and held Three Moons high overhead. The fighting faltered and stopped as the men watched to see the outcome of this amazing fight. Which man would reach Suleiman first? They held their collective breath for an unendurably agonizing few seconds.

Draco had never tried to fight at such speed before. Not only did he have to kill his enemy before the man reached Suleiman, he would have only a fraction of a second in which to strike his blow. His timing would have to be absolutely perfect. Suleiman straightened at the sound of hooves thundering down upon him from two sides. He did not stir from where he stood.

At the last possible instant, the desert man knew that he was not going to be able to strike Suleiman before the big Frank was upon him. Quick as a snake, he used the scimitar to cut at Draco's face, just as Three Moons came down in a blow so swift and so powerful that it could scarcely be seen. The watchers saw the two men come together, saw the scimitar flash across, saw a vague, silver blur as Three Moons came down, and heard a sound like a huge ax cleaving a tree. Then the two men were past one another, and it seemed as if no contact had taken place. At last, the watchers let out their long-pent breath as, with horror and wonder, they saw the black-robed desert raider fall from his horse in two pieces, one to each side of the beast, divided cleanly from crown to crotch. A moment later, the saddle fell away, likewise cleft.

The remaining raiders groaned their dismay. "God is great!" shouted Osman, and the guards fell upon their demoralized enemy so fiercely that they were disposed of within minutes.

When Draco had his horse back under control, he walked it slowly back to where Suleiman waited. There was no rush now, and he didn't want to ruin so splendid a beast. As he rode, he cleaned the blade of Three Moons with a corner of his robe, lest the blood ruin the fine polish of her sides. Anxiously, he checked the priceless edge, which had been sharpened when it left the smith's shop and had not been touched by a stone since. Miraculously, it seemed to have suffered no harm despite the terrific use to which it had been put.

Osman and Wulf and some of the other guards were standing around their master, expressing their joy in his preservation. They fell silent as Draco dismounted and dropped to one knee before Suleiman. "Forgive me, master," Draco said, holding forth the sword. "I couldn't reach my own sword and was forced to use Three Moons."

He remained kneeling with his head bowed as Suleiman took the fabled blade and examined it carefully for damage. At last he said: "She seems not to have suffered from the experience, although you used her with a redundancy of force. Stand up."

"Master," said Osman, furious with indignation, "why did you leave our protection? Rahman is your guard and pledged to die in your defense. How could he have faced his God thinking that you had been killed trying to save him?"

"Rahman was bleeding to death from a wound that

was simple to bandage," Suleiman said, "and the day of my death is written upon my brow like any other man's."

Osman and Draco looked at each other in commiseration. Their master's unshakable belief in kismet, the inevitability of fate, was the despair of his bodyguards.

"Now," Suleiman said, "let us go over to the oasis and rest by the cool water. Bring the wounded carefully. I trust you took some of the raiders alive?"

"Three, master," Osman said.

"Do you know their tribe, Osman?"

"Bedouin of Wadi al Hakim," he said, spitting ostentatiously. "Dogs and slaves with the hearts of women. They will cut your throat for an old pair of sandals, since they could never make anything so demanding for themselves. Their tribe was sired on a sick jackal bitch by a vulture who employed the vomit of a pox-ridden maggot for semen. On nights when their women are out raiding graves for corpses to eat, the men fornicate with lepers in order to spread their kind throughout the world."

"They gave you and your men a good fight," Suleiman observed, smiling to himself.

Osman shrugged. "Shaitan gives them strength, since their sexual and dietary habits give him such delight."

When they were seated by the water the men began bathing their wounds, carefully drawing the water into basins and helmets and washing at some distance from the spring so as not to defile it with blood. Wulf blotted at Draco's face with a damp cloth. The leader of the attackers had opened up his face from the right inner edge of his coif to the nose, missing the eye by half an inch. The travelers who had been at the oasis flocked around them with gifts of food and bandages to bind up their wounds. They explained how the raiders had held them prisoner to keep them from going ahead and warning the oncomers that an ambush lay in wait. Now, Suleiman was questioning the three attackers who still lived. They had no reluctance about telling him who had sent them.

At Dhat al Hajj, Suleiman had uncovered evidence of graft and corruption by the governor. This man and others on the pilgrimage route had been growing rich by selling protection to the pilgrims; protection that was supposed to be given freely. He had sent word by fast courier to his cohort in Mahtab. That worthy had found this pack of desert vipers and hired them to ambush and kill the whole party before they made more trouble. Suleiman nodded at this recitation, sad but resigned to the evil ways of his fellow man.

"I could forgive you for trying to kill me," Suleiman said to the three. "It is a crime so often attempted that I have come to regard it as a minor offense. However, your crime is much graver. You have attacked pilgrims on the *hajj*, and there is only one punishment for this."

He nodded, and a small group of his men led the three raiders away from the oasis, toward the site of the battle. Draco stood and followed them, unsheathing Three Moons, preparatory to carrying out one of his duties as Suleiman's sword bearer. It was not one that he minded particularly. His master never condemned men to death save for the foulest crimes, and there could be no disgrace in executing men who had attacked pilgrims.

When Draco returned to the oasis, men were chattering volubly, boasting of their valor in the day's battle and showing off their souvenirs. A big black Sudanese of the guard held up the divided saddle, split so neatly that it might have been done by a joiner's tool. Another had both halves of the Bedouin leader's helmet, and two others had one half each of his silvered mailshirt. As Draco passed, they called out to him and showered him with praise as the hero of the day.

Personally, he was beginning to feel the letdown that usually followed such frenetic action. The cut on his face was beginning to throb. It would, of course, be infected by tomorrow. He had aches and pains where he had been struck when he had not bothered to defend himself, but there seemed to be no broken bones. He found Suleiman off meditating by himself. Uncharacteristically, the old man smiled warmly as Draco approached. He held out his hands in a familiar gesture, and Draco placed Three Moons, complete with sheath and belt, in them.

"A fine blade, isn't she?" Suleiman said, hefting her weight. "You've seen how terrible she can be." He looked at the sheathed sword, seeming lost in his memories. "I was your age when I took her from the dead hands of my father. My own sons are dead now, and I am growing too old to wield her." Suddenly, he thrust the beautiful weapon back into Draco's hand. "You will practice with her every day under my supervision. From this day forward, I will not hold her again." The old man turned and left Draco standing, stunned, with Three Moons in his hands. She was his, just as Suleiman had said she would be, years ago. Unbelieving, he ran his hand over the long grip, knowing that he and the sword would never be separated, except by death. He looked up at the crescent moon and smelled the perfume of the date palms. With this sword, he would accomplish the vengeance he had sworn for his father, and for the betrayed Crusader army that had died at Hattin.

Falcon's mutterings woke Constance. She still lay upon his chest, his arms were still around her, and their bodies were still joined as they had been at the moment of ecstasy. His hands were moving in an odd caressing motion.

"What are you dreaming about?" she murmured. "What are you doing with your hands?" She nearly purred her enjoyment of the delicious sensations.

Falcon was half asleep. She had difficulty making out his muttered words. Finally, she understood. "Loveliest thing I've ever felt," he was saying.

She smiled and laid her head back on his chest, filled with a complacent satisfaction. She would have been infuriated to know that his words referred not to her velvet flesh, but to the rough, sharkskin-bound handle of a sword.

ELEVEN

They set out in the first gray light of dawn. The horses clopped patiently, the oxen endured their age-old burdens with the equanimity of their kind, and the wagons creaked and screeched with protest. So early in the day, there was nobody to bid them farewell but the guard who opened the city gate. The morning was gloomy and overcast, with a promise of a chill rain in no great time.

To Falcon, the knowledge that this miserable mission was drawing to its close was almost enough to make up for the unpromising aspect of the day. Ten more days, or thereabouts. Out of the mountains, free of the threat of being trapped by snowfall or avalanche, able to meet predators on more even terms, it did not seem like so long.

What would he do after making his contact and delivering the treasure? He would have to find a place for the men to winter. Perhaps some pleasant coastal city that needed a strong garrison against troublesome neighbors. He had been born near the sea and he was tired of living inland. Besides, there were great advantages to having access to a port. News traveled faster by water than over land. At a port like Marseilles, frequented by ships of a dozen nations, he could have news of Alexandria or Constantinople before he heard of the latest doings in Paris.

He could charter galleys to ferry his men and supplies wherever they were needed. Sea travel was hazardous, but as this journey had amply demonstrated, travel by land was far worse, as well as being slower. As he considered it, the idea seemed more and more attractive. Perhaps a stint on the Mediterranean was just what they needed. The climate was far better than in the north, the barons were just as divided and disputatious, and, more important, they were far richer.

He would look into the situation in Italy and Sicily, made inquiries about the Papal States and the communities of North Africa. His men would have no objection to serving a paying Saracen as long as it wasn't against Christians, and many of them wouldn't even draw the line at that.

There were other attractions to the plan. There were fine orchards. There was a good wine all year around. The ale-drinkers would not be so pleased, of course. Ale was rare in the South. Well, he couldn't expect to please everybody. The roads would be clear most of the year, and there would always be plenty of fodder for the animals. Finding winter clothing would cease to be a problem of logistics. He had been present at sieges that had turned into disasters when winter appeared too early and caught the besiegers in their summer gear.

Wulf broke in on his musings. "What are you brooding about, my lord?"

"I was thinking we ought to set up down by the sea someplace," Falcon answered. "I'm tired of the rain and fog and snow. We lived too long in Outremer, and it spoiled me."

"That would be pleasant," Wulf agreed, nodding. "I'll miss the ale, though."

"We'll set up our own brewery," Falcon said. "We've men who know the craft. I prefer wine, anyway. There are plenty of beekeepers in the south. Don't you Saxons drink honey mead?"

Wulf grimaced. "Honey mead is awful stuff! We only drink it when the ale runs out."

"It's a small price to pay when you consider the advantages," Falcon maintained.

"The South it is, then, my lord," Wulf concurred.

Fulk and Bors rode at the head of their men along a road that led through a wooded area of sweet-smelling pines and poplars. They had ridden around Falcon and his army on the night they had spent in the town. For six days, they had ridden ahead at a leisurely pace, and now they were well into the lands of orchard and vineyard. As they came to a bend in the road, they saw that a barricade had been erected. Lounging around the barricade were a dozen armed men.

The men leaped to their feet when the bandits came into view. One of them, armed better than the rest, raised a hand. "Halt and state your business!" he called.

"Out of our way, lout," Bors said. "You can't stop us."

"Probably not," the man said, "but you wouldn't care to encounter our master, who awaits a little way down the road. If you have anything of value, you'd better hand it over now and we'll let you have safe passage."

"This is a bold one," said Fulk with a chuckle. "It strikes me that only one man could be his master."

"I serve Enguerrand the Rapacious," the man said.

"Go and fetch your master," Bors said. "Tell him that Fulk and Bors are here and we have a proposition for him that will be to his great profit." The guard spoke to one of the others, and that one mounted and rode off down the road.

A short time later, a sizable force of men arrived at the barrier. At their head rode a pale, cadaverous, wasp-thin man in excellent armor. Beneath the rim of his helmet, his face was as fine-drawn as an ascetic saint's. The cheekbones were high, with the ivory-colored flesh stretched so taut over them that it seemed about to burst.

"Greetings, my friends," Enguerrand said in a voice like the whispering of ghosts. "What brings you to visit me?"

"Business, Enguerrand," Bors said. "Did our messenger not reach you, weeks ago?"

"Doubtless he fell prey to some misfortune of the road," Enguerrand answered. Bors had little doubt of the kind of misfortune his man had encountered, but he let it pass. Enguerrand dismounted, and the brothers did likewise. They followed Enguerrand to a tree, where he seated himself on a bed of pine needles and gestured for them to join him. Although he appeared to be frail, Enguerrand moved under the weight of his armor as lightly as if he were dressed in court clothes. In battle, Bors knew, Enguerrand wielded an ax heavy enough to strain the wrist of all but the strongest men.

"What is the nature of this mission?" Enguerrand asked.

Quickly, wasting few words, Bors and Fulk acquainted him with what they knew of the treasure and of Draco Falcon.

"With your men and ours combined," Bors said, "we can take them right here when they pass your barrier. It will be a hard fight, but we outnumber them by a goodly margin."

"Not here," Enguerrand demurred. "This is not a good ambush spot. There are too many trees, and the action could easily split up into scattered running fights over which we would wield little control. I know a better place."

"Good, good," Fulk said, with admiration. "I knew that with you on our side, we could not fail. Did I not say so, Bors?"

"You did. All know of the craftiness of Enguerrand the Rapacious, the master of stratagems."

Enguerrand accepted this praise with a courtly nod. "I learned my trade well in Outremer, as, it seems, did this Falcon." Outremer, which meant simply "Oversea," was the common name for that area of the Middle East over which the Crusades had been fought. "I learned early that war is more than a matter of strong arms and stout hearts."

"Where do you propose that we take them?" Fulk asked eagerly.

"You say that this chamberlain serves the Viscount of Limoges?"

"He said so," Fulk answered.

"I suspect that the man is a rogue who wished to do his master an ill turn, and that the treasure actually belongs to this viscount."

"What causes you to think that?" asked Bors.

"Because the treasure train is headed straight for a fief called Forêt-St.-Denis, which belongs to that same nobleman. Doubtless this Falcon has been hired to escort it to that destination."

"How far is that?" Bors asked.

"A day's ride," Enguerrand answered.

"Then we must strike quickly," Fulk said.

"We will make our move with due consideration," Enguerrand said. "On this road, the boundary of Forêt-St.-Denis is marked by a bridge over the Gorge of Lost Souls. That is where we will meet them. In the meantime, we must make arrangements. I want you two and your men to remain here, well in the forest and hidden from view, until Falcon and his men have passed. Fall in behind them and follow closely, but do not risk battle." The brothers nodded assent.

"I," Enguerrand continued, "shall send a man to Forêt-St.-Denis to tell the seneschal that the train has been delayed and will be arriving in about a week. That will give us a free hand at the border." Fulk and Bors looked at each other and nodded in admiration of this cleverness.

"And the division of the loot?" Fulk asked.

"That we can discuss when we know what we've taken," Enguerrand said. Fulk and Bors readily assented. Enguerrand, of course, had no intention of sharing any loot. Neither had they.

Falcon was riding by the wagons when the Welshmen arrived to render their report. With him were Bishop LaCru, Wulf, and Ruy Ortiz. Today Rudolph had the van and Sir Andrew commanded the rearguard. "The men who were ahead of us have split up," Ruy said. "They've ridden into the woods and still hide there."

"They're letting us pass by," Falcon said. "They must want to fall in behind us again, but why?"

Sir Ruy's face twisted in unaccustomed thought. "Front's a better position. If they want to be behind, they must think they control our front. Are you sure that all of them have taken to the woods? Might they have sent a force on ahead of us?" Falcon noted the Spanish knight's analysis with approval. He had been trying for years to get his men to think beyond sword's reach, and at last it seemed to be paying off.

"Most of them, for sure," said Gower ap Gwynneth. "But there've been others staying in this area until no later than yesterday, more than a hundred of them, by the signs, and those moved out ahead."

"By God's wounds!" Falcon swore loudly. "The bastards have linked up with another pack of brigands. They're going to catch us in a nutcracker, with armies before us and behind." He continued to swear luridly for some minutes. His companions waited in respectful silence as he vented his spleen in several languages. At last, he lapsed into ill-tempered silence.

"Very good, my lord," Wulf said at last. "Rupert at his best couldn't have topped that last one. Blasphemy won't help us, though. What do we do now?"

"Why not just proceed as we have been?" Ruy said. "We're in good country for fighting. Even if they outnumber us, they're just outlaws. Surely we can take care of any such."

"They won't try to take us in open country," Falcon said. "They're going to catch us at that damned bridge."

"The bridge!" Ruy said, his eyes lighting up. Falcon knew what the Spanish knight was thinking. Nothing would be more heroic than a single knight defending or forcing passage of a bridge. The tale of Horatius had not been forgotten, and the nameless Viking at Stamford Bridge was still sung of in England and Scandinavia. "Sir, please let me have the honor of being first onto the bridge."

"My advice," said Bishop LaCru, "is that we ride on a little way, then turn around and attack the men following us. Once we've destroyed them, we can go ahead and deal with the enemy in front."

"That's exactly what I'd do," Falcon said, "if it weren't for the damned wagons. They must have spies watching us. We'd have to abandon the wagons for a while when we turned to deal with the followers. The others would come in and take them while we were occupied."

"Where does that leave us?" LaCru said.

"Just where we were before," Falcon said. "Headed for that bridge with enemies before and behind."

They rode on, while word was passed that action was imminent. The men reacted almost with relief. The journey had been a period of frustration and discontent for them. They were proud of their professional abilities but they had been able to call them into play very little lately. Normally they had boundless confidence in their leader, but he had been as stymied as they on this mission. Worst of all, they had been tempted by the presence of the treasure into mutinous thoughts against the leader to whom they had sworn fealty, and who had always acted toward them with the most scrupulous adherence to the rules of feudal loyalty, just as if they had been as wellborn as he. This made them feel guilty, and, with the sublime illogic of men looking for a scapegoat, they blamed it on the bandits who had been plaguing them. The prospect of an open fight, to end the suspense one way or the other, made them positively cheerful for the first time since setting out on the ill-starred venture.

Falcon heard with satisfaction the sounds of men readying themselves for battle. The clink of arms, the creaking of leather straps being tightened, the voices of men making wagers on who would be bravest in the coming fight, all were infinitely preferable to the sullen mutterings and silences of recent days. He rode to the wagons and rapped on the side of Constance's conveyance. She and Suzanne stuck their heads out.

"The men sound happy," Constance noted. "Why is that?"

"They're going to be fighting soon," Falcon said, smiling.

"Not again!" Constance said. "Who is it this time?"

"The same bandits, plus some new villains they've recruited. I'd say we'll be outnumbered by quite a bit."

"Send ahead to this man de Burgh," Constance advised. "He'll send reinforcements."

"I'd like to," Falcon said, "but the new bandits hold the bridge we have to cross to reach de Burgh. We'll just have to fight it out. I hope it won't come to it, but you should be prepared for capture. I suppose you know how it's done by now. De Burgh is your uncle's liegeman, so you shouldn't be in captivity for long."

"You won't let them take me, Draco," she said confidently.

He wished that he could share her confidence. "I shall do my best to keep you safe," he said.

"Don't take any unnecessary risks," she counseled. "You have knights and soldiers to do the fighting. You are a commander and your task is to oversee things, not to endanger yourself needlessly." This was alarming talk, Falcon thought. She was already sounding like a wife.

"Put up your shutters and keep your heads down for now," Falcon said. "I'll see you again when all is safe." He had had Rupert furnish the women's wagon with stout wooden shutters to shield them from stray missiles during conflict. They commended him to God, and he rode to the head of his troops.

There was a long, gentle slope from the top of the bluff, then an area of flat ground, then the Gorge of Lost Souls. The land ended abruptly at the edge of the gorge, leaving a sheer drop of hundreds of feet. The bridge had been built at its narrowest point. It was no more than fifty paces long, but it was narrow. The good Roman masonry had withstood the centuries splendidly, though some stones had fallen from the low walls that flanked the roadbed.

Falcon's little army stood in a compact mass at the top of the bluff. Around Falcon were Wulf, LaCru, and Falcon's knights. They surveyed the gorge grimly. "No sign of men yet," LaCru said.

"They'll be there soon enough," Falcon answered. He looked around and signaled Guido of Genoa to join them. "Guido, take your crossbowmen and the archers and put half on either side of the bridge on the lip of the gorge. Concentrate your fire on enemies on the other side or on the bridge. Try for men who look like leaders, but for God's sake, don't kill any horses on the bridge or we'll never get across."

Guido nodded and called his men, and the little band of missile troops rode ahead of the van. The rest started down the slope at a slow pace.

They were no more than halfway down the slope when men rode out of the treeline on the far side of the bridge. "Get ready," Falcon said.

"They could be de Burgh's men," LaCru said hopefully.

"Not damned likely," Falcon answered.

"Men behind us!" Wulf called, loud enough for his master to hear through the muffling coif. Falcon turned in his saddle and looked back up the slope. A mass of mounted men were arranged along the bluff where Falcon's men had been just a few minutes before. Among them he could discern Fulk the Devil. At a walking pace, the bandits began to descend the bluff. The other force was already at the bridge. When they were at the near end of the bridge, Falcon's army came to a halt. Falcon and his knights rode to the front to parley. Wulf rode at Falcon's back and LaCru was with them, his club at the ready.

From the other side rode a thin, pale-faced man who was plainly the leader. "I am Enguerrand, sometimes called the Rapacious. Surrender your treasure wagons to me and you may proceed unmolested."

The answer was terse. "I'm Draco Falcon. Get out of my way or I'll kill you." The other showed no sign of moving. Falcon turned to the knight who rode on his left. "Here's your chance, Ruy," he said. "Kill that man."

Without further ado, Ruy Ortiz lowered his lance and charged onto the bridge. With a slight gesture, Enguerrand signaled to one of his men, and another robber-knight thundered onto the bridge with lance couched. The hooves of both chargers struck sparks from the stones of the roadbed, and both forces held their breath for long seconds. Ruy's lance point caught the other man's shield dead center. It smashed through the tough wood and nailed the man's left arm to his side. The Spanish knight halted his horse and hoisted the robber-knight into the air on the end of his lance like a speared eel, hurling him into the abyss below.

A huge cheer arose from Falcon's men. "Forward!" Falcon cried, spurring his horse. Then he was on the bridge with his Saracen sword out and his shield up. Ahead of him, Ruy Ortiz was hacking men down with the cold, methodical skill of the born swordsman. A man on horseback forced his way past the Spaniard and tried to lance Falcon, who leaned aside and made a precise cut above the edge of the other's shield. The man rode on, minus his head. Then the press of horses was such that the men of both sides could only stay in their saddles and flail away at any enemy who chanced within arm's reach.

By holding the far end of the bridge, it was clear that Enguerrand intended to let Fulk and Bors do the bulk of the fighting from the rear. The brothers had ordered the charge at the commencement of hostilities, and they were now heavily engaged with the rearguard. Under orders, Rudolph of Austria and Sir Andrew of Scotland made their way to the rear to take charge. They found that their well-drilled men were holding formation as they retreated slowly toward the bridge. The two knights began barking orders to keep the men steady. A fighting withdrawal is the most difficult of all maneuvers, and a slight break in formation could lead to panic and rout.

Surrounded by his tight-packed men, Falcon was unable to reach any enemies, so he stood on his saddle to survey the chaotic scene. Behind him, the rearguard was engaged but orderly. Ahead, Ortiz and LaCru were fighting side by side and had forced their way almost to the far end of the bridge. Frequently, he would see a bandit topple, felled by the bolts or arrows of Guido's missile troops. He resheathed the curved sword and took up his ax, which was a better weapon for this kind of close work. He heard a loud cry from ahead, and he looked up to see his men pouring across the bridge to the other side. Oritz and LaCru had forced their way across, and now Falcon's men, supported by the bowmen, were making a secure area on the other side.

Falcon took up his hunting horn and blew a prolonged blast. This was the signal for the wagons to come forward onto the bridge. The force in the rear seemed to be larger and more dangerous than that in front, and Falcon didn't want the wagons to linger on that side longer than absolutely necessary. As his men began to pour over the bridge, the wagons creaked and groaned their way onto the stone roadbed.

Fulk the Devil, seeing the wagons roll onto the bridge, howled at his men to redouble their efforts. Let those wagons fall into Enguerrand's hands, he knew, and they were lost forever. Under the relentless fury of the assault, Falcon's retreating men began to give way. Gaps were appearing in the line, and wounded horses were beginning to force their panic-stricken way through the men who fought on foot. Wherever these gaps occurred, the bandits were quick to exploit them. The defense began to fall apart.

Falcon saw the disorder in the rear, but he was unable to make his way back to it, so dense was the pack on the bridge. He jumped from his saddle to the wall along the bridge and began walking back toward the rearguard action. He found many knots of his men making separate stands at the lip of the gorge, while Rudolph and Andrew held the entrance to the bridge itself. Both were dismounted now, Rudolph swinging his heavy sword, Cheeseparer, while Sir Andrew was striking seemingly in all directions with his combination poleax. Falcon jumped from the wall and hewed a man down with his ax. "Rally to me!" he called. A few men began to make their way to him, but most could not. Then a clamor behind him made him turn around. The wagons were stalled, and it seemed that bandits from Enguerrand's army were forcing their way onto the bridge in spite of the best Falcon's men could do.

"Hey, you, Falcon!" It was a burly man Falcon recognized as Fulk the Devil. "Truce! I'll help you kill Enguerrand and his men and we split the treasure. Agreed?"

"I'll feed you to the crows, bandit!" Falcon shouted. He jumped back atop the wall and made his way back toward the wagons. Cursing, Fulk ordered two of his men to attack Sir Andrew. While the Scottish knight was engaged, Fulk bulled his horse past him and onto the bridge. Some of his men followed as he began to fight his way to the wagons.

Falcon felt some of the ancient stones shift beneath his feet as he walked along the top of the low wall. Then he saw another man walking the wall toward him. It was Enguerrand the Rapacious. Enguerrand was making his way toward one of the wagons which was stalled on the bridge. The crowd on the narrow structure had forced the wagon against the wall, where it sagged dangerously as its oxen bellowed in panic and strove to break loose from their traces. Atop it, he could see Rupert Foul-Mouth challenging all comers with his heavy maul.

"Come and get it, ye pig-pronging pukelouse," Rupert shouted at a bandit who strove to climb the wagon. The big wooden hammer fell and the bandit dropped with his helmet smashed down between his shoulders.

Then Rupert caught sight of Enguerrand. "You, too, wheyface!" the old man called. "Come in reach of me little hammer and your goat-fucking days are over!" By now there was no semblance of order anywhere, as soldiers and bandits fought indiscriminately at both ends of the bridge and upon it. Whatever they had been fighting for to begin with, treasure, honor, or duty, they were now fighting to live or simply to kill. A true madness seemed to have overcome most of them, and some of the bandits were actually fighting the brigands of someone else's band.

Falcon reached the wagon at the same time as Enguerrand. The pale knight chopped low with his ax, aiming at Falcon's knee. Falcon lowered his shoulder and caught the blade on the point of his shield, aiming in return an overhand blow to Enguerrand's helmet, which the other likewise caught on his shield. The two sprang apart, swaying for balance atop the narrow wall.

As will sometimes happen in battle, a lull now occurred. As if by common consent, the exhausted men broke off engagement and backed away from one another for a breathing spell while two of the champions fought it out. All turned to watch the bizarre duel on the bridge wall.

Crouched behind their shields, Falcon and Enguerrand approached one another cautiously. With a sudden spring forward, Enguerrand threw a looping overhand blow aimed to split Falcon's helmet. Instead of raising his shield as expected, Falcon leaped violently toward the pale knight and smashed his shield against Enguerrand's. Throwing his arm completely around his enemy, Falcon jerked his ax around, snapping in at the wrist to bring the heavy edge crashing into Enguerrand's back over the kidney. He felt the mail rings crunch inward. Whether the armor was broken made no difference. Enguerrand arched back, half his internal organs ruptured by the blow. Falcon gave him a shove with his shield, and Enguerrand toppled from the wall to smash into a shelf of rock which protruded from the wall of the gorge thirty feet below.

There was silence for several seconds. Before Falcon's men could raise a cheer, the oxen pulling the wagon broke loose at last, and the heavy vehicle sagged against the wall. Falcon felt the stones beneath his feet lurch sickeningly. "Ware the wall, my lord!" shouted Rupert, jumping clear of the lurching wagon. Falcon leaped as hard as he could, to come down upon a mixed knot of soldiers and bandits, bringing some of them tumbling to the roadbed.

All watched unbelieving as, with slow and stately dignity, the wall crumbled and the wagon soared gracefully out into the empty air. With an unbelievable crash, it burst to a thousand pieces on the rock ledge, directly atop the remains of Enguerrand the Rapacious.

Falcon got to his feet and walked to the gap in the wall. Not only the wagon but the chests within it had been smashed. Hundreds of flat, rectangular plates glinted silver-gray in the sunlight. To his amazement, Falcon realized that Fulk the Devil and his brother Bors were standing next to him, studying the wreckage of the fallen wagon. Rupert came to join them, then others. Nobody seemed inclined just yet to resume the fighting.

"Silver plates," said Fulk, bemused. He scratched his beard. "I'd've thought it would've been gold."

"Silver plates your louse-bitten, pustulent old arse!" Rupert shouted, pointing down at the heap of metal. "Them's lead roofing plates! I've roofed enough castles in my day to know. We've all been gulled and gulled proper, by damn!"

All the men still standing gaped in sheer disbelief. It was impossible. They *couldn't* have toiled and fought all over these long, weary days and miles for a few wagonloads of leaden roof tiles! It was just too much.

Falcon found Wulf standing beside him now. Others were making their way to him: Donal and Rupert, Guido, Simon and Gerd, the Welshmen, the knights. All were thinking the same thing: Who would try to kill Falcon first, the bandits or his own outraged men? They gripped their weapons until the tension became unbearable.

It was Fulk who began the laughing. The silence was shattered by the bandit chief's howls of mirth as he leaned over and slapped his armored thigh. "Lead! We've been fighting for lead! That's the best one I've ever heard!" Hesitantly, the mood of hilarity spread from man to man, bandit, soldier, and knight, until within minutes every man still alive and not too badly wounded was rolling on the ground with tears streaming down his face, holding his sides and helpless with laughter. It continued for several minutes. The laughing would almost die out, then someone would break into fresh peals and the rest would be off again.

The women looked out from their wagon to a scene of seeming mass madness. They had been hearing the frightful sounds of battle, then silence, then a stunning crash, and now this. It was just too strange, and they prudently retired back inside.

When all had laughed themselves into complete exhaustion, the brothers Fulk and Bors came to where Falcon sat on the roadbed with his back against a wagon wheel. "We'll bid you good day, Sir Draco," Bors said. "Maybe we'll see you again when you have something worth taking, but I sincerely hope not. We're going to go find a good place to set up. Would you care to join us?" Falcon, too exhausted to speak, just waved them away. The living bandits mounted and rode off.

"Rupert," Falcon called. "Raise that lead and distribute it among the other wagons. I promised to deliver it, and that's what I'll do."

Sir Maurice de Burgh looked at Falcon without comprehension. "Lead? You say you've come halfway across France to deliver some wagonloads of lead?" He scanned the contract Falcon had handed him. "I was told of no treasure, nor of any lady being sent here. Yet this is my liege's seal."

"You were not told," Falcon said, "because it was never intended that either treasure or lady were to arrive. We were sent as a decoy while the real treasure, if indeed it exists, travels by some other route, probably by sea. With this deception, he cleared his realms of bandits, who were all chasing us. As for the Lady Constance, his own niece, her convenient death would place her lands back at his disposal."

169

"Sir, you impugn my liege!" said de Burgh angrily. They sat at a table in one of de Burgh's castles.

"I'll kill your liege if I ever see him," Falcon said. "But if you need more proof, I have it." He turned to Wulf. "Bring that wretch in."

Wulf left and returned a few minutes later with Jean the Chamberlain, much the worse for his stay among the bandits.

"I know you," said de Burgh. "Are you not one of my lord's servants?"

"I am, Sir Maurice. My lord sent me to go ahead of this knight and his train, telling all the villains I could find of the great treasure that was to be had by attacking it."

Sir Maurice looked slightly sick. "I will, of course, accept care of the Lady Constance, and see to it that she arrives safely at her husband's home in Italy."

"I said I'd deliver her here, and that I've done. Whether she wishes to stay is up to her," Falcon said. "Now we must open all these chests and weigh out the lead."

"Weigh it?" said Sir Maurice. "Whatever for?"

"Because one-tenth of it is the papal tithe." He turned to LaCru. "Is it not, archbishop?"

"It is," LaCru said grimly. "I shall personally deliver it to the Holy Father, and tell him of the man who sent it and caused the deaths of so many."

Falcon sat in the chamber that de Burgh had put at the disposal of Lady Constance. For a long time, she had been reluctant to discuss serious matters. Now she broke a long silence.

"I won't go with you, Draco," she said at last.

"That is probably the right decision," he said, very slowly.

"For all its hardship, this has been a glorious adventure," she said, the words coming very fast now. "I've loved a shining knight out of a poem, but poems don't last a lifetime. It would be a life without land, without friends, with unending travel and no home for me or our children if anything should happen to you. I would hate it and in time I would come to hate you because of it. Like the knights in the poems, why don't you just ride away, and I'll wave at you from my tower window." She would not look at him.

Falcon got to his feet. He took her hand and kissed it. "In that case, my lady, I wish you all happiness with your future husband. Pray he's not a warrior." He turned and left the room. Constance cried for a long time afterward with her head pillowed on Suzanne's shoulder.

As they rode away from the castle, Falcon did not look back to see if she was waving. He looked sad, but not as grim as Wulf had expected.

"We're never lucky with women, are we, my lord?" Wulf said.

"Maybe that kind of life isn't for men like us," Falcon said. "Come on, Wulf, let's go find the sea."

They wheeled their horses and rode south.

The following is an action-packed excerpt
from the next novel in this
sword-swinging new Signet series set in
the age of chivalry:
THE FALCON 5: GREEK FIRE

Six men lurked in an alleyway between towering, decaying tenements. A heavy fog had come off the sea with the setting of the sun, and it would soon be impossible to see. The inhabitants of Messina had never heard of street lighting, and one ventured out of doors after dark at one's mortal peril. The lowest galleries of the sulfur mines not far from this city were not blacker than the nighttime city itself.

The men were hard-bitten rogues, all heavily armed. Two wore rusty shirts of mail, and all carried swords and daggers. "Someone coming!" hissed one.

All drew a little deeper into the shadows as two men trod warily along the street onto which the alley opened. The lurking men studied the newcomers. "Are they the ones?" asked one.

"Must be," said the man who was leading them. "See the white blaze on the taller?"

As the two drew closer it could be seen that they were both big men, dressed in ordinary hose and tunic. Nothing else about them was ordinary, however. The taller was a hawk-faced man with a complexion burned brown by exposure, with flint-gray eyes and black hair. Through the hair, from brow to nape, ran the white streak the cutthroat leader had remarked upon. Across

173

the black-haired man's back was sheathed a long, curved sword of Saracen make. Its grip protruded over his right shoulder and was long enough for two hands.

The other was half a head shorter, but still taller than most men. He wore a steel cap, and long locks of unruly yellow hair spilled from under its rim. At his belt was slung the kind of short, curved sword called a falchion, and on his back he carried a small round shield of iron, much dented and scarred. Both men walked warily, their eyes darting restlessly, scanning all the dark doorways and alleyways in their path.

"They don't look easy," said one of the cutthroats.

"We were told they wouldn't be," said the leader. "Still, they're only two against six. We're being well paid for our risks."

The leader was not as confident as he wanted to sound. They had been hired to ambush a Northern knight and his man-at-arms. He had expected a couple of bumpkins from the rural, barbarous northlands: men at home only on horseback or defending some castle. These two were plainly on familiar territory, just as confident on a foggy street as they would be in camp or castle.

"Now!" whispered the leader. All six darted into the street. Three took up positions before the two victims, three behind. The two big men stopped, wary but not at all amazed or afraid.

"What's it to be?" said the taller. "Our purses? Our lives?"

"Which do you think?" taunted the cutthroat leader.

"It makes little difference," said the man with the white blaze. "You'll get neither."

"In and kill them!" barked the leader. All six footpads jumped forward at once.

The two "victims" reacted with incredible speed and decision. The taller reached behind his shoulder and whipped out the long, curved sword and in the same motion brought it down to the left in a huge arc that halved an unarmored man from shoulder to waist. At the bottom of the arc, he twisted the sword dexterously and brought it back upward to the right, catching a mailed man beneath the jaw, splitting his skull from chin to eyes. The leader darted in, thrusting with his short sword, only to feel its point grate against the mailshirt beneath the tall man's tunic. His last sight of this world was that of the heavy bronze pommel of the curved sword, shaped like a crescent moon. It smashed into the bridge of his nose, jamming splinters of bone into his brain. He was dead before he struck the filthy cobbles of the street.

While the black-haired man engaged the three attackers in front, the yellow-haired one spun on the balls of his feet so that he guarded the other's back and vice versa. He had the falchion in his right hand and the little shield in his left so quickly that he was on guard before he had stopped turning. The biggest of his attackers stepped in swinging a long sword with both hands. The other two had to step to the rear to give their companion room to swing his weapon. Instead of blocking the ponderous sword, the yellow-haired man dropped to one knee as he parried the blade upward, causing it to slide by harmlessly over his head. He made a short, horizontal slash that gutted the swordsman, then he was back on both feet.

The remaining two cutthroats had to leap over the body of their late friend, and the blond man used their momentary imbalance to sweep his blade across the throat of one. The other darted in, trying to stab the yellowhair beneath his sword arm with a dagger, only to receive a boot in his midriff. As he bent over in agony, the little shield came down on the back of his neck, snapping it like a twig.

The two men stood in the little circle of bodies in the midst of a sudden silence. From the commencement of the attack to the fall of the last man, no more than a dozen heartbeats had elapsed.

"Did you leave one alive?" asked the taller man.

"No, my lord," said the other. "Didn't you?" The taller shook his head. They both cleaned their weapons with scraps of cloth cut from the corpses.

"I wish I knew who they were," said the man with the white blaze. His name was Sir Draco Falcon, and he was the captain of a free company.

"Probably just common robbers," said the yellow-haired man. He was a Saxon and his name was Aethelwulf Ecgbehrtsson, but for many years he had gone by the shortened form of Wulf. He had been Falcon's companion since boyhood.

"I hope so," Falcon answered. "If not, then our contact wasn't being as secret in his business as he thought." They had come here from Palermo to receive a commission under conditions of utmost secrecy.

"Should we report this to someone?" said Wulf.

"Why bother?" Falcon said. "Thieves will strip them and dump the bodies into the bay. Let's go on back to the inn."

The inn where they had left their companions was a two-story structure near the wharves. The lower floor was given over to a kitchen and common room where travelers could eat and drink at long tables and pass out on the straw-covered floor. The upper floor consisted of a single large room, and Falcon had rented this room to house himself and the twenty men he had brought down from Palermo. The rest were garrisoning a castle for the governor of Sicily. The island had been conquered by the German emperor a couple of years before, and it was still a little agitated.

Wulf and Falcon crossed the common room and climbed the ladder that led to the loftlike room. Inside, they found their companions sitting about on their traveling bags, drinking wine, dicing, and swapping lies in the immemorial fashion of off-duty soldiers in all climes and periods.

One looked up as they came in. He had a hideously scarred face and only one ear. "Did you find your man?" he asked. He was Donal MacFergus, an Irishman by birth and an ax fighter by trade. Except for Wulf, Donal had known Falcon longer than any other man of the company.

"We did," Falcon answered. "He gave me this." He held up a folded piece of parchment from which dangled a seal. "And this." He tossed Donal a merrily clinking pouch. "And he took his leave."

"Strange doings," commented a sandy-haired man. He was called Simon the Monk because he had lived in a monastery before taking up the soldier's profession. "What's the parchment say?"

"I'm about to find out," Falcon said. With his dagger, he cut the ribbon from which the seal dangled. He tossed the seal to Simon. "Recognize it?" Falcon asked.

Simon studied the waxen disc. It depicted a winged lion with one forepaw around a cross. There was lettering around the periphery, but, as was usual with small seals, it was quite indecipherable. "The lion of St. Mark," Simon said. "The Venetian Republic?"

"So I suspect," said Falcon. By the light of the flickering torch, he worked his way through much florid Latin which said, in essence, that the Most Serene Republic of Venice wished to hire his services. The bag of gold was earnest money and traveling expenses. He was to present the parchment and seal to any Venetian ship on its homeward journey from Messina to receive passage to Venice. As he translated, he read this out to his men. In one corner sat his crossbowmen, all dressed in studded leather jerkins. Their expressions grew more alarmed with each passing word. Finally, one of their number got to his feet and strode over to where Falcon pondered over the missive.

"My lord," the leather-clad man said, "surely you don't propose that we go to Venice!"

"Why not?" Falcon said. "They seem to wish our services and I've never heard that Venetian gold was inferior to any other."

"Because we're all Genoese," the man said, gesturing to himself and the other crossbowmen. "They'll string us up by the balls in that city. We've been at war for centuries. Besides, they're all liars and thieves and cheats. Best to avoid them, my lord."

"Guido," Falcon said, "you don't serve Genoa. You serve me. Do you wish to leave my service?"

"Why, of course not, my lord. It's just—"

"Rest assured, Guido, I shall not allow the Venetians to harm you. Now, go sit down." Chastened, the Genoese rejoined his companions.

"Who sent this commission?" Simon asked.

"Not the whole damned senate, I'm sure," Falcon said. "But there's no personal seal affixed, just the lesser seal of the Republic." Then his eye chanced upon something unfamiliar at the bottom of the parchment. It was a name and title, written in a bold scrawl that contrasted sharply with the clerkly hand of the message. In a largely illiterate age, signatures were a rarity and seals were the rule. This was why Falcon had not noticed it at once. He read out the Latinized name.

"Henricus Dandalus, Dux. Who the hell is that?" he wondered.

"Enrico Dandolo, the doge himself!" wailed Guido. "The devil incarnate! We're doomed!"

The Venetian roundship was a broad-beamed vessel with sails that filled with the wind, round as the bellies of pregnant women. Falcon stood in the prow with the salt spray in his nostrils watching the dolphins play hide-and-seek with the ship. He had not been at sea in years, and he found it a welcome change from the hard riding, marching, and fighting that had occupied his recent life. He was a wanderer by nature, and had come to resent the way his army, which he had built and trained with such loving devotion, tied him to one spot for months at a time.

In the waist of the ship, the crossbowmen sat in a dispirited group, halfheartedly gambling and feeling more like prisoners than soldiers. Donal and Wulf were enjoying the voyage, but Simon was stretched out on the deck near the centerline of the ship, greenish in color and preparing for the life to come. Two tall bowmen sat near him, their six-foot bows of yew carefully wrapped against the damp. They were from Wales and had no more use for the nautical life than had Simon. The ship's crew made traditional fun of the landlubbers and studiously ignored the Genoese. They had taunted their rivals at first, but Falcon had thrown a few of them overboard and now they minded their manners.

The ship's master came forward to where Falcon watched the dolphins. He pointed to a low island in the distance. "That's the Lido," he reported. "On the other side is Venice. We'll tie up around midday." Falcon nodded absently. He had never seen Venice. To hear its inhabitants speak, it was the New Jerusalem. Falcon had seen the old one and had not been terribly impressed. He doubted that Venice could compare with Antioch or Alexandria or Damascus and certainly not with Constantinople. He had visited all of those places, and anything the West had to offer was invariably shabby by comparison.

The city turned out to be an agreeable surprise. Relatively new by Mediterranean standards, it lacked the dilapidated air of most cities. The usual clutter of livestock was absent, and the city did not smell nearly as bad as most. Falcon and some of his men wandered delightedly among the squares, crossing bridges over the narrow canals and exploring the markets and taverns.

Conspicuously absent from Venice was the aristocratic class of Western Europe. Built on the sea, Venice had no arrogant landowners. Instead, its aristocracy was a new type of man: the merchant prince. Instead of broad estates, his fortunes were composed of ships, warehouses, and goods for trade. His livelihood came from the sea, and it could be precarious. A sudden storm could wipe out a family's fortunes in a matter of minutes.

Falcon established his men at an inn which overlooked the Grand Canal and dressed himself in his best clothes. He considered wearing armor for the sake of the intimidating impression it invariably made, but he was never at ease wearing a great deal of iron around so much water. When he was satisfied with his appearance, he went in search of the doge.

Enrico Dandolo, the Doge of Venice, sat in his heavy, thronelike chair in the office where he spent at least sixteen hours of most days tending to the affairs of the Republic. He was nearing seventy, but his frame was still powerful and vigorous. He wore a coif of black velvet, and the long hair which hung beneath it was as snow-white as the beard that flowed over the breast of his rich robe. Flanking the beaklike nose were a pair of brilliant blue eyes. He turned to face the door as his personal secretary entered.

"The barbarian is here to see you, excellency," the secretary said.

"Barbarian? Which one?"

"The Norman knight you summoned a few weeks ago. He's arrived in Venice today and craves audience."

"What's he like?" Dandolo demanded.

"Not as crude as most," said the secretary fastidiously. "He speaks well. I suspect that he has spent some time among civilized people. Very tall, with big hands covered with scars and calluses. His coloration is rather strange."

"How so?" Dandolo asked.

"He's dark as a Saracen, but his eyes are pale gray. His hair is black and straight, but he has a plume of white hair running in a streak from front to back. A thin, white line runs down his face from the bottom of the streak. Down his neck as well. The line crosses his eyebrow and turns it white there. He frightens the secretaries and scribes in the outer office. They're all clutching amulets and making signs. They think he has the evil eye."

"Superstitious fools," Dandolo said. "That man's been marked by lightning. How old is he?"

"Middle thirties, I would say. He has all his teeth. That's rare in soldiers." The secretary was accustomed to furnishing the doge with these detailed reports, and had learned the arts of reading a man's appearance without appearing to.

"Send him in," the doge ordered.

"He carries a huge sword and refuses to surrender it," the secretary warned.

"If he surrendered his sword he wouldn't be the man I want," the doge said. "Let him keep his sword. Don't disturb us while we confer." The secretary left and returned a few minutes later.

"I present Sir Draco Falcon, excellency."

When Falcon came into the room, Dandolo turned his face toward him. Falcon found himself looking into the brightest blue eyes he had ever seen in a human face. The gaze transfixed him like a serpent's. He had never felt such personal force radiating from another man. This ancient patriarch was the embodiment in human form of the power of the will.

The secretary left without bowing and closed the heavy door behind him. "Sir Draco," Dandolo said, "please be seated." He gestured toward a chair which faced his own. Falcon found himself sitting uncomfortably close to the old man. He guessed that this was a ploy the doge used to unsettle those he had to deal with.

"Sir Draco, I trust you are able to keep a secret."

"As well as any man," Falcon answered.

"You have a good voice," Dandolo said, surprisingly. "Are you familiar with the sea?"

"I've spent a good deal of time on the sea," Falcon answered.

"You don't volunteer much information," Dandolo said.

"No," Falcon agreed.

"Very well. I have a mission of utmost importance which must be undertaken by a person not of Venice, and not known to be in the service of the Republic. It requires a man of very rare qualities."

"Such as?" Falcon queried.

"Can you read?"

"Yes," Falcon said.

"Getting information from you is like pulling teeth," Dandolo said. "Latin only?"

"Latin, French, Arabic, and Greek," Falcon said.

"This surpasses expectation. Turkish?"

"No," Falcon admitted, "but I speak it tolerably well."

"Have you ever had dealings with Constantinople?" Dandolo asked.

"I once served in the emperor's army."

"Do you feel any lingering loyalty?"

"I served for pay," Falcon said.

"At sea or on the land?" asked Dandolo.

"On land. Cavalry and infantry both."

"And you were a Crusader, I take it. How else would you have learned Arabic and Turkish?"

"I spent much of my youth in Outremer," Falcon said. Outremer, which meant "Oversea," was the common name for the lands where the Crusaders battled in the East.

"Excellent," Dandolo said. "And where did you gain your experience upon the sea?"

Falcon smiled grimly. "I pulled an oar for two years in a Turkish galley."

"Were you ransomed or did you escape?"

"I was freed," Falcon temporized. This was an area of his life he did not wish to discuss. Dandolo caught his reluctance and smiled.

"Very well, I won't press. Give me your hand!" Dandolo held forth his own. Mystified, Falcon placed his own hand in Dandolo's big-knuckled talons. The doge turned the palm upward and ran the fingers of his other hand over the calluses. "Yes, this is an oarsman's hand, no question of that." Then he reached out and ran his hand over Falcon's face. "Your face matches your voice. I am sure that you are the man we need."

Falcon's surprise was followed by sudden comprehension. No wonder the servant hadn't bowed as he left. For all his brilliant blue eyes, Enrico Dandolo, doge of Venice, was blind as a stone.

Dandolo sat back in his chair once more. "To business, then," he announced. "Sir Draco, what do you know of Greek fire?"

"I've heard of it, of course," Falcon said. "I never saw it in use. It's the emperor's secret weapon, has been for centuries. It's mainly used by the navy, I heard. The army never used it while I was in the emperor's service."

"With good reason," Dandolo said. "On land, one of their projecting machines might be overwhelmed and the secret of the fire discovered. A ship can be scuttled before that could happen. Every Greek captain who carries it has orders to sink his own ship before risking the loss of the Greek fire. No other nation has managed to capture a projector, a supply of the Greek fire, or the formula for its making." The doge's ancient face took on a faraway look.

"In my youth, when I had two good eyes, I saw it used once. I was second in command of a galley of the Republic. We were at war with Constantinople and our squadron of four ships encountered a crippled galley lying up in shallow water after a storm. She was in a bay on the eastern end of Crete. She seemed to be easy prey.

"As the first of our galleys neared her, I saw a long tube being lowered from the mast like a crane. We knew what was about to happen, but it was too late to save that first galley. *Pegasus* was her name, and her captain tried desperately to ram and board. I saw men aboard the Greek galley working over some mechanism. It appeared to be a pump. A long stream of fire emerged from the tube. *Pegasus* didn't just burn. She was instantly engulfed in a cloud of terrible flame. The heat

184

was so terrible that it scorched the sides of our ship, a hundred paces away." Falcon sat enthralled by this account of the world's most feared and terrible weapon.

"The *Centaur* attacked next, from the side opposite the tube. The Greek galley launched clay pots of the Greek fire by catapult. A dozen fires broke out on the *Centaur*. My own vessel went alongside to help fight the fires, but it was no use. We took off as many of the survivors as we could, and left the *Centaur* to burn.

"My own ship, the *Serenissima*, and the other, *Bellero-phon*, backed away and blocked the harbor. That night, we sent six small boats to attack the Greek ship all at once. There was no way they could use the fire. I had to remain aboard the *Serenissima*. We heard the clash of arms for a few minutes, then there was a terrible flash of light: a fireball like the sun at noon, with a sound like thunder or a great volcano in eruption. The Greek captain had obeyed his orders.

"The next morning, we combed the bay and the shore for survivors. All our brave sailors who had been on the boats had perished. We had scarcely enough left to take our two remaining galleys back to Venice. On the shore, we found one Greek sailor, badly burned but still alive. He wore a curious amulet around his neck. It depicted three men in the midst of flames, by which I took them to be Shadrach, Meshach, and Abednego, who walked unharmed amid the flames. I was sure that this was one of the men who served the flame weapons."

"Did he speak?" asked Falcon.

"He died within the hour," Dandolo said. "He never regained consciousness."

"Unfortunate," Falcon said. "You might have gotten some answers from him."

"I doubt it," Dandolo answered. "He was tongueless.

We found the burned bodies of three others with the amulet. All were tongueless."

"I think the Greek emperor means to keep the secret of his weapon," Falcon observed. "How do I fit into all this?"

"I have been contacted by a Byzantine official," Dandolo said. "He is turning coat. For the last five years, he says, he has been in charge of the place where the Greek fire is made. He will sell us the secret, in return for a great sum of money and asylum in Venice. If we do not respond within the month, he will make his offer to the caliph."

"Who is this man?" Falcon asked.

"He did not come in person, of course. He sent an agent."

"You realize, of course, that he's almost certainly made his offer to the caliph already," Falcon said.

"Of course he has," Dandolo said testily. "I didn't get to be doge by being stupid. That's why I want a fighting man who knows the sea."

"And one who doesn't work for another maritime power," Falcon said.

"Exactly," Dandolo concurred. "It is good to talk to a soldier who is also politically astute. It's a rare experience."

"Who is this agent the turncoat sent you?"

"I was just coming to that." Dandolo pulled a cord that was hung by his chair. A door disguised as a cabinet swung open and a figure in heavy black robes entered. Astonished, Falcon rose slowly to his feet.

"Sir Draco," said Dandolo, "I have the pleasure of presenting Lady Anna Theodosia."

About the Author

MARK RAMSAY was born on St. John's Day, 1947. He is a professional writer and he lives on a remote mountaintop in the Appalachian Mountains. When not writing, he pursues his lifelong study of the Medieval and Classical periods. He makes his own weapons and armor and sometimes fights with them, when he can find someone to practice with. He feels this brings a breath of authenticity to his writing.

JOIN <u>THE FALCON</u> READER'S PANEL AND PREVIEW NEW BOOKS

If you're a reader of <u>THE FALCON</u>, New American Library wants to bring you more of the type of books you enjoy. For this reason we're asking you to join <u>THE FALCON</u> Reader's Panel, to preview new books, so we can learn more about your reading tastes.

Please fill out and mail this questionnaire today. Your comments are appreciated.

1. The title of the last paperback book I bought was:
   TITLE:_____PUBLISHER:_____

2. How many paperback books have you bought for yourself in the last six months?
   ☐ 1 to 3   ☐ 4 to 6   ☐ 7 to 9   ☐ 10 to 20   ☐ 21 or more

3. What other paperback fiction have you read in the past six months? Please list titles:_____
   _____
   _____
   _____

4. My favorite is (one of the above or other):_____

5. My favorite author is:_____

6. I watch television, on average (check one):
   ☐ Over 4 hours a day   ☐ 2 to 4 hours a day   ☐ 0 to 2 hours a day
   I usually watch television (check one or more):
   ☐ 8 a.m. to 5 p.m.   ☐ 5 p.m. to 11 p.m.   ☐ 11 p.m. to 2 a.m.

7. I read the following numbers of different magazines regularly (check one):
   ☐ More than 6   ☐ 3 to 6 magazines   ☐ 0 to 2 magazines
   My favorite magazines are:_____
   _____

For our records, we need this information from all our Reader's Panel Members.

NAME:_____
ADDRESS:_____
CITY:_____STATE:_____ZIP CODE:_____
TELEPHONE: Area Code (   ) Number_____

8. (Check one) ☐ Male   ☐ Female

9. Age (check one): ☐ 17 and under   ☐ 18 to 34   ☐ 35 to 49
   ☐ 50 to 64   ☐ 65 and over

10. Education (check one):
    ☐ Now in high school   ☐ Graduated high school
    ☐ Now in college   ☐ Completed some college
    ☐ Graduated college

11. What is your occupation? (check one):
    ☐ Employed full-time   ☐ Employed part-time   ☐ Not employed
    Give your full job title:_____

Thank you. Please mail this today to:

THE FALCON, New American Library,
1633 Broadway, New York, New York 10019